NORWALK PUBLIC LIBRARY

WITHDRAWN
NORWALK OHIO

9780803 49 2233

D1711680

OCT 96

ELIMA

(Book Five)

A HOLLY ST. JAMES ROMANTIC MYSTERY

NORWALK PUBLIC LIBRARY
NORWALK, OHIO

ELIMA
(Book Five)

•

GEORGETTE
LIVINGSTON

AVALON BOOKS
THOMAS BOUREGY AND COMPANY, INC.
401 LAFAYETTE STREET
NEW YORK, NEW YORK 10003

© Copyright 1996 by Georgette Livingston
Library of Congress Catalog Card Number: 96-96753
ISBN 0-8034-9223-5
All rights reserved.
All the characters in this book are fictitious,
and any resemblance to actual persons,
living or dead, is purely coincidental.

PRINTED IN THE UNITED STATES OF AMERICA
ON ACID-FREE PAPER
BY HADDON CRAFTSMEN, SCRANTON, PENNSYLVANIA

For all the guys behind the badge,
who have made my job easy

Glossary

'AE: Yes
AHUI HO: Until we meet again
AIKANE: Friend
ALOHA: Greetings, welcome, farewell, love
ALOHA AU IA OE: I love you
A'OLE: No
HAOLE: Caucasian, white
HAOLEKANE: White man
HOLOMU: A long, fitted dress; a combination of a holoku and a muumuu, long but without a train
HO'OLAULE'A: Celebration
IMU: Underground oven
KAMA'AINA: Native-born
KĀNE: Man, husband
KAPU: Forbidden
KEIKI: Child
LEHUA: Flower of Pele
LLIKAI: Surface of the sea
MAHALO: Thanks
MAIKA'I: Fine
MAKE: Dead
MUUMUU: Loose dress; Hawaiian version of the missionary "Mother Hubbard"
NANI: Lovely
PILIKIA: Trouble
PUPU: Hors d'oeuvre
TUTU: Grandmother
WAHINE: Woman, female, girl
WAIANAPANAPA: Glistening water
WIKIWIKI: Fast

Chapter One

"So, did you get her name when she called?" Holly asked, trying to get the zipper up on her flowered sundress.

"Uh-huh, but it's six dozen letters long, so everybody calls her *Tutu*. That's grandmother in Hawaiian. She's a *kama'aina*, a native-born islander, and supposedly has good references." Logan sidled up behind his wife and began to nibble on her shoulder. "You want some help with your zipper?"

Holly leaned against him, loving the feel of his warm, sultry kisses against her sun-bronzed skin. "Mmm, but remember, the zipper goes up, not down. So what happens if she has a prune face, like the last one?"

2 *Georgette Livingston*

"Then I guess we'll have to try again." Logan sighed. "I had no idea finding a housekeeper was going to be this difficult."

"Hiring a housekeeper was your idea, not mine," Holly reminded him. "And you're the one who keeps finding fault with all the applicants."

Logan groaned. "Okay, tell you what. When she gets here, take her out to the terrace. I'll supply a pitcher of lemonade and coconut cookies, and leave the two of you alone. If you like her, that's all that matters."

Holly looked up at him slyly. "Bet you'll be peeking around the corner."

"Maybe, but I won't embarrass you. Though I'd appreciate a thumbs-up or down when you decide."

"How about a wink? Two winks for yes, one for no?"

"And how am I going to be able to see a wink if I'm inside the house?"

"Well, you can make your presence felt, off and on. You know, check to make sure we have enough cookies. Water a plant or two on the terrace. Did you tell her she'll be doing most of the cooking, too?"

Logan kissed the tip of Holly's nose. "I told her you can't boil water, so I usually do the

Elima 3

cooking, but now that I'm going to be busy with the Bali Hai project . . .''

"Logan!"

Logan chuckled. "Just teasing, sweetheart. I told her, and she was happy to know her outstanding culinary skills would be put to good use."

"That sounds arrogant."

"Well, that isn't exactly the way she put it."

"Did you tell her we have a security gate down on the road?"

"I told her."

"And did you tell her she's going to have to go through a maze of cane fields to find the house?"

Logan rolled his eyes. "I've done this before, sweetheart. In case you've forgotten, this is the fifth applicant. Why don't you relax, and go read a book or something?"

"I'd like to do 'something' better. We still have a couple of minutes before she gets here . . .''

Logan's golden-brown eyes were filled with love as he gathered Holly in his arms. "Bet I'm in for it now," he said huskily. "Mushy stuff."

"Forever and ever and even after that," Holly said, raising her face for his sweet kiss.

A few minutes later, Holly was on the ter-

4   *Georgette Livingston*

race when Logan escorted prospective house-keeper number five through the double sliding glass doors. Tutu nearly defied description. She had a round face, rosy cheeks, warm brown eyes, and dimples everywhere—at the corners of her mouth, across her knuckles, at her elbows, and Holly bet if she peeked under the rotund little lady's full-length muumuu, she would find dimples in her knees. She wore zori sandals on her stubby feet, and three garlands of kukui beads around her neck. And there was no way to estimate her age, even though her close-cropped, wiry hair was gray. She had one of those timeless islander faces, which meant she could be anywhere from her early forties to late sixties. And the best part was the kooky straw hat she had perched on her head, reminiscent of an upside-down fruit bowl topped with flowers.

Holly liked her immediately, and was delighted with her singsong way of talking, which incorporated authentic Hawaiian, English, and a sprinkle of pidgin.

"*Nani*," Tutu whispered softly, looking out across the pool to the ridge, and then at the purple-hued mountains beyond.

"Yes, it *is* lovely," Holly said, winking twice at Logan to let him know Tutu was perfect, and he could relax.

Elima 5

A few minutes later, Logan brought out a pitcher of lemonade and a plate of coconut cookies, kissed Holly's cheek, and made a hasty retreat. But she could see the look in his eyes. *"Don't make up your mind until you see her references!"* he said with his glance.

A few minutes later, Holly looked at the woman's references. They weren't only good, they were impeccable.

Holly poured lemonade into two tall, frosty glasses and said, ''Your references are outstanding, Tutu, but I'd like to know a little bit about you as a person. I take it you aren't married?''

''My husband is *make*, dead,'' Tutu said. ''Many years now. I have one *keiki* who is grown. He is a fine young man who lives on Lanai with his wife and son. When I am not working, I live with my sister in Lihue.''

''Does it bother you that we live so far away from everything?''

Tutu waved her arms. ''Our island of Kauai is not that big, and I have a truck. It runs *wik-iwiki*.''

Holly smiled. ''Okay, so it runs fast, but does it run well?''

'' '*Ae*.''

''Perhaps I should tell you a little bit about us . . .''

6   *Georgette Livingston*

"I know enough. I can tell you are much in love and live a happy life."

"You're very perceptive, Tutu, but I think I had better tell you what I do for a living. I'm a private investigator. My brother and I own St. James Investigations. Our father left us the business when he died, and we've worked very hard to make it the best it can be."

Tutu grinned, displaying very white teeth against the dark sheen of her skin. "You are a P.I. like Magnum, yeah. Good TV show, o' wot? You drive a red car?"

Laughter bubbled up. "No. I used to drive a chuggedy Chevy Nova until I was in an accident. Now I'm driving a white Blazer."

"Too bad. You would look good driving a red car. That happen in the accident?" Tutu was nodding at the scars on Holly's arm.

"Yes, but not in *that* accident. I know I should think about having plastic surgery, and maybe I will someday, but right now the scars are a reminder of how precious life really is, and how quickly it can be taken away." Holly took a deep breath. "My husband is a semi-retired DEA agent."

"DEA?"

"Drug Enforcement Administration." When Tutu shook her head, Holly went on. "He was forced into an early retirement after somebody

Elima 7

slashed his back with a knife. There was a lot of spinal damage, and they didn't think he would ever walk again. But he fought the odds. He's supposed to be fully retired, but he's still involved with the department. I thought you should know about our crazy lifestyle . . . Well, the job is yours if you want it, Tutu, but I don't want you to be upset if you see a gun, or if the house is suddenly swarming with cops.''

The grin broadened. ''A Fed like Eliot Ness, o' wot?''

''Well, sort of. Logan keeps his weaponry under lock and key, but you probably should know the rest of it. He has state-of-the-art surveillance equipment in the wine cellar, an escape route at the back of the garage, and a helicopter landing pad just north of the ridge. He has also installed a high-quality security system around the house, that includes an intercom system. That way, nobody gets through the front gate unless we want them to. If any of this bothers you . . .''

Tutu shook her head. ''It bothers me only a little.''

''Good! And I want you to understand our life isn't all cops and bad guys. A lot of my cases are nothing more than a paper chase, and Logan has many other interests. Just recently, he completed a very special project. He owns

8 *Georgette Livingston*

ten acres on a bluff near here, and has turned it into a park.''

"The *Ho'olaule'a* Park?''

"Yes, the 'Celebration' Park. Then you've heard of it.''

" '*Ae*. Everybody has heard of it. Your husband is an *aikane* to the land. A good friend to the land.'' Her dark eyes were gazing off in the distance again, and her sigh was whisper soft. "This is the most beautiful house I have ever seen, Mrs. West, yeah. I will be happy here. I will be happy working here.''

Holly shook the woman's plump hand. "And we are a very happy to have you.''

"*Mahalo*,'' Tutu said.

Pleased with her choice, believing she had hired a true gem, Holly said, "I'll take you on a tour of the house and your quarters, and then perhaps you'd like to go to Lihue and get your things?''

Tutu gave Holly a dimpled grin. "My heart told me this would be a good job. *My* job. I brought along a box. It will be enough for now, yeah. Mr. West said I would have a kitchen.''

"Yes, you do have a small kitchenette, but it was put in only as a convenience for you. We want you to think of this as your home, like you are a part of the family, and that includes eating your meals with us.'' Holly

Elima

9

sighed. "Unfortunately, things are a little disorganized right now, and we can't always find the time to share the dinner hour. If you have trouble with that . . ."

Tutu gave Holly an impish smile. "I will make sure there is always much food in the house, and that you will always find time to eat—"

Tutu's words were cut off by the sound of voices in the house, and then distinctly, "Oh, boy, I didn't realize you guys had company."

Cindy Tolover had stepped out on the terrace with Logan, and gave Holly an apologetic smile. "Sorry."

Holly smiled at her best friend. "Don't be silly. You haven't interrupted anything. Tutu, this is Cindy Tolover, gift shop/art gallery owner extraordinaire, and a very good friend. Cindy, this is Tutu, our new housekeeper."

The women shook hands, and Tutu's dark eyes flickered over Cindy's soft, coffee-colored hair and trim figure appreciatively. "*Nani,*" she said finally.

Holly smiled. "Yes, she certainly is."

Cindy flushed, and murmured, "*Mahalo.*"

Logan spoke up. "Come along, Tutu, and I'll give you the grand tour while Holly chats with her friend."

10 *Georgette Livingston*

"I would like that," Tutu said, following Logan into the house.

Cindy sat down and sighed. "I know I should have called first, but . . . Well, I knew you were going to be home today. She seems really sweet."

"Tutu? She's wonderful, and I practically hired her on the spot. How about a glass of lemonade?"

Cindy shook her head. "I don't think I could keep it down."

Holly eyed Cindy intently. "I *knew* something was wrong the minute you walked through the door."

Tears welled up in Cindy's hazel eyes. "I didn't want to bother you, but Danny is on Oahu at a security convention—that's what happens when your fiancé is the director of security at a big hotel—and my mother is on Maui shopping till she drops with my aunt, who is visiting from the mainland. They always go a little crazy when they get together . . ."

"And?"

"And . . . you remember all those wonderful paintings I have hanging on a wall in the gallery?"

"By the Italian beach bum artist?"

"Yes. Marty Ricco. Gorgeous seascapes and

Elima 11

swaying palms. He has a way of capturing the island's beauty with wonderful, feathery strokes and so much sensitivity . . .'' She bit at her lip. ''Well, apparently Marty went wind surfing with some friends, and . . . Well, they were at Anini Beach. The surf was too high, so he was the only one who went out. He didn't come back, Holly. The rescue team found his sailboard, but no sign of Marty.''

''Oh, Cindy, that's terrible! Does he have a family?''

''That's what the police wanted to know. He never gave me an address, and his friends weren't any help. They said they met him on the beach, and that's where the friendship stayed. But one of them remembered Marty saying he was an artist, and that his work was in a local gift shop with an attached art gallery. There are only a couple of setups like that on the island, so the police found me in a blink. And boy, did they unload the questions. Now, I don't know what's going to happen. If he's dead, the paintings will be part of his estate, and it's so sad. Such a waste. He was so talented.''

''What did the police do with the paintings?'' Holly asked.

''They were going to take them, but decided they didn't have room for them in the property

12   *Georgette Livingston*

room. So they took inventory, to make sure I don't sell any of them, I guess. As if I would! They dusted the paintings for fingerprints, too, but wouldn't tell me why.''

"It's simply a way of identifying him, Cindy. A name is a name, and can be changed, but if his fingerprints are in the police computer, they might be able to get an address and locate his family. If he's not in the computer, I would imagine the next step would be the Department of Motor Vehicles. When did this happen?''

"The surfers reported it yesterday morning, and the police questioned me yesterday afternoon. I almost called you, but I had such a headache, I closed up early and went home. The police said they'd keep in touch, but you know how that goes. I have the feeling they aren't going to give this top priority. Meanwhile, I have to think of a way to tell my customers the paintings are no longer for sale.''

"And they still haven't found the body?''

Cindy shrugged. "I have no idea. Nothing in the paper. Nothing on TV or on the radio, and I know I'd get the runaround if I called the police station.''

Holly was trying to figure out the best way to handle it, when Logan returned to the terrace carrying a plate of sandwiches. "That lady is

Elima **13**

a wonder. She made these while I was giving her a tour of the kitchen. Now, she's talking about making a lemon meringue pie.''

''Mmm.''

''That's what I said.'' He looked at Cindy and frowned. ''Uh-oh. I don't like that look.''

Holly quickly told him what had happened, and added, ''Do you think you could call Max Kentaro, Logan? He might have some answers.''

Logan picked up the cordless phone, punched in some numbers, asked to speak to Lt. Kentaro, and waited. Finally, ''Yeah, Max, it's Logan. You know anything about an alleged drowning at Anini Beach? Happened yesterday morning. A guy was wind surfing . . . That's the one . . . Still haven't found the body, huh? What about family? No family that you know of. Okay, address? Come on, Max, *somebody* on the island must know where the guy lives. I know. Cindy Tolover is here now. We know about the paintings. Are you going to question his friends again? Yeah, well, don't you think it's strange the body didn't wash up on the beach? Uh-huh, I know how the currents are, and I know how he could be tangled up in seaweed twenty feet under . . . I know, Max, you're short on manpower . . . I understand that, too. You've asked the media to put a lid

14 *Georgette Livingston*

on it until after you've located his relatives. And if you don't? What about fingerprints on the paintings? No fingerprints? Don't you think that's strange too? I know . . . Right. Thanks, Max. Keep in touch.''

Logan punched the OFF button, and sighed. ''You two catch any of that?''

Holly said, ''Enough to know they haven't found the body, or his relatives, they don't know where he lives, and they didn't come up with any fingerprints on the paintings. They might not think that's strange, but I do. Did you ever see Marty touch the paintings, Cindy?''

Cindy thought for a minute, and shook her head. ''He always brought the paintings into the gallery wrapped up in butcher paper. I was the one who unwrapped them, and hung them on the wall. He never stuck around either. Quite literally, he was a man of very few words.''

''But he had to handle the paintings before he wrapped them up,'' Logan reasoned. ''Kinda makes you wonder if he painted with gloves on. I know, that's a ludicrous thought.''

Holly said, ''Or he wiped the paintings off. How did you meet Marty Ricco, Cindy?''

''It was about a month ago. He walked in one day with a painting, and wanted to know

Elima 15

if I was interested in trying to sell his work. I thought at the time that was a strange way to put it. I knew I wouldn't have to try. The paintings would sell themselves. It occurred to me he wasn't aware of his own talent. The painting was a gorgeous Hawaiian sunset, and tourists love that sort of thing. I asked him if he had any other paintings, he said he did, and over the next few days, he filled up my wall. I had twenty to start with; now I have ten.''

''Did you see him after that?'' Holly asked. ''I mean, how did you handle the money end of it?''

''I saw him a week ago. I paid him for the paintings I sold, less my ten percent, and he promised to bring in more paintings.''

''But he didn't.''

''No, he didn't. And now . . . Darn! It makes me so angry. All that talent wasted, and for what? If his friends thought the surf was too high to go in the water, why didn't he listen to them? Why did he have to be the idiot!''

Logan managed a comforting smile. ''You can't do anything about it, Cindy, so why don't you try to relax. Max said he'd keep in touch.''

Holly patted Cindy's hand. ''And you can begin by staying for lunch.''

Cindy stood up, and shook her head. ''I have an appointment with a supplier at one, so I'd

16 *Georgette Livingston*

better get going. Call me if you hear anything?''

''Promise. Come on, I'll walk you to your
car.''

''And I'll take a peek in the kitchen,'' Logan
said, giving them a sheepish shrug. ''So, what
can I say? Old habits die hard.''

Holly looped her arm through Cindy's.
''He's talking about cooking, not snooping,
though he's pretty good at that, too.''

Holly's comment finally put a smile on
Cindy's face, and it was as welcome as the
Hawaiian sun.

Chapter Two

"I'm totally pampered, and outrageously lazy, Jack. Right now, I'm out on the terrace, drinking a frosty glass of iced tea while languishing in the sun, and enjoying every moment of my day off. And that's what happens when you finally find *the* perfect housekeeper. Her name is Tutu; that's grandmother in Hawaiian. She's only been here a few hours, and we're already beginning to wonder how we ever got along without her. She looks like Hilo Hattie, and quite literally, fills every corner of the house with sunlight. She's always smiling and singing, and bubbles over with warmth, love, and enthusiasm. At the moment, Logan is in the kitchen, patiently waiting for her

18 *Georgette Livingston*

yummy lemon meringue pie to come out of the oven.''

''Uh-huh, so you finally found a housekeeper who fits Logan's stringent requirements, did you? Well, congratulations.''

''You sound like you're in a mood, Jack, or maybe even bored.''

''I guess you could say I'm a little bit of both. That's why I called. I wanted you to know I'm closing up early. Not much going on here, so I might as well be home, helping Kim with the kids.''

''Nothing came in today at all?''

''Besides bills? Just a lost husband who turned up on Maui after a weekend toot.''

At that moment, Logan walked out on the terrace, carrying a tray containing two pieces of pie. Holly gave him a wink, and squeezed his knee. ''Well, tell Kim 'hi,' kiss the kids for me, and—''

Jack interrupted with, ''Whoops. A pretty lady just walked in. Keep your fingers crossed she isn't selling Avon, and needs a P.I. See ya.''

''See ya,'' Holly said.

Logan placed the plates on the table, and kissed Holly's forehead. ''I've already had a taste, and I can tell you now, you're in for a treat.''

Elima 19

Holly took a bite, and rolled her eyes. "This is heavenly!"

"Told you. Did you tell Jack about Cindy and the artist?"

"Didn't have the chance. He was busy giving me all the reasons why he was going to go home early, and then a woman walked into the office, and—"

Holly's words were cut off by the ringing phone. Logan took the call, then frowned. "It's Jack," he said, handing Holly the cordless. "Sounds like he's in a bit of a mess."

Holly put the phone to her ear, and could hear hysterical weeping in the background. Jack had to yell over the din. "You remember the pretty lady who walked in while we were on the phone a few minutes ago? Well, her husband is missing. One morning he went to work, and didn't come home. That was three months ago."

"And?"

"And, that's it. That's all I've been able to get out of her. She's really in a bad way, Holly, and you know how I get when I'm around hysterical females. Makes me want to jump into a volcano. I know this is a lot to ask, but I thought if you could talk to her, calm her down . . ."

"Put her on the phone."

20   *Georgette Livingston*

"No, I mean in person. She needs to see your friendly face."

"Why don't you refer her to somebody else, Jack? That sounds like the best solution to me. Try Ed Barns. The last I heard, his agency is floundering, so I'm sure he would appreciate the business."

"We can use the business, too, Holly. Many more months like this one, and we'll be floundering around with Ed Barns. She said I could name my price. She doesn't care how much it costs as long as I find her husband."

Holly sighed. "Well, I guess it wouldn't hurt to talk to her, if you can hang on until I get there."

Jack's voice brightened. "Piece of cake if I know you're on your way. Thanks, Sis. If Logan has a fit, tell him I won't keep you tied up for hours. Just long enough to get her settled down."

Holly rang off, and gave Logan a helpless shrug. "Did you get the gist of that?"

"Not really," Logan said with a scowl. "But I know you're going to the office."

"Only for a little while. Jack needs some help with a potential client. Her husband is missing, and she's in a bad way."

"And Jack can't handle it?"

"Well, I suppose he could if he had to, but

Elima 21

he's never been good around weepy females, and this one is really hysterical.''

Holly finished her pie in a couple of healthy bites, and got to her feet. ''I know, my love,'' she said, wrapping her arms around Logan's neck. ''This is supposed to be my day off, but I don't see anything wrong with helping my big brother out of a pickle. And I promise, I'll be home before five, when you have to leave for your meeting. I mean, we wouldn't want to leave Tutu alone on her first day.''

Logan groaned. ''The meeting with Bob Dolan and the planning commission. I'd forgotten about it, or maybe I wanted to forget about it.''

''But you know how much the Bali Hai project means to you, and to Kauai's future. We need that kind of cultural center, and they need your input.''

''But that's just it. They aren't listening to my input, and frankly, I'm getting tired of all the arguments.''

''Well, then, you're just going to have to make them listen.'' She struck a pose. ''Do I look okay? Or should I take the time to change?''

She was wearing white slacks and a fluffy pink blouse and had her red hair in a thick braid down her back. Logan's golden-brown eyes twinkled, and he gave her a seductive

22　　　*Georgette Livingston*

wink. "You look wonderful, sweetheart. Be careful."

She gave him another hug. "I will. See you at dinner."

St. James Investigations was on the second floor of a well-established professional building in Lihue. The office was small but efficient, and overlooked a courtyard filled with tropical flowers. There had been many times over the last several years that Holly and Jack had talked about moving into a larger complex, but they knew they could never go through with it. The little office they shared was where their father had started the detective agency many years ago, and there were simply too many wonderful memories.

Holly walked down the hall, waved at an attorney coming out of his office, and took a deep breath before she opened the door. She stepped in, and placed a professional smile on her face.

The woman was still weeping, hunkered over in a chair, with her face in her hands.

Jack was sitting behind his desk, and jumped up. "Ah, there you are! I told Mrs. Rocettie you handle most of the missing-person cases, Holly, and that she really should talk to you. I told her this was your day off, but that you

Elima 23

were willing to help out. I also told her you live a good distance away, so it might take some time for you to get here . . ." He was babbling, extremely flustered, and ran a hand through his dark red hair. "This is my sister and partner, Mrs. Rocettie. Her name is Holly. Holly, this is Anna Rocettie."

The woman looked up at Holly with red, swollen eyes, and shook her hand, though it was more like a frantic grasp.

Jack cleared his throat. "Ah, well, I think I'll run down to the bakery and get a dozen doughnuts. Maybe some cookies, too. Give you ladies a chance to talk." He handed Holly the file. "This is what I've got so far. The coffee is fresh if you want a cup. Okay, I'm out of here."

After Jack hurried out of the office, Holly sat down at her desk, waited a few moments for the woman to compose herself, and took inventory. Anna Rocettie had dark hair and eyes and a pretty, heart-shaped face—classy. Designer jeans and expensive white blouse. Leather boots and handbag. Gold chain necklace. Diamond earrings. Gold wedding band on her ring finger. Probably in her mid thirties.

Finally, Holly opened the file, and looked at the three sparse entries: *Anna Rocettie. Husband went to work, didn't come home. Hasn't*

24 *Georgette Livingston*

seen or heard from him in three months. It was the same information Jack had given her on the phone, so it was obvious he hadn't gotten any further.

Holly smiled at the woman, and said, "I hope you aren't upset with my brother for asking me to help out, but to be honest with you, he's never been very good around distraught females."

Anna Rocettie sighed, and dabbed at her eyes. "Please, call me Anna, and I understand. I'm so embarrassed . . . My husband hated to see me cry, too." Tears filled her dark eyes again, but she choked them back. "I wanted to be adult about this, but when I got off the plane . . . I love my husband, Miss St. James, and I miss him so much."

"When you got off the plane?"

"Yes. I felt so alone, yet I just knew Mario was on the island. I could *feel* it. I went to a phone booth and looked under 'Private Investigators,' and was so glad to see there were only a couple. I closed my eyes and pointed. My finger landed on St. James Investigations." She shrugged. "I know that's not the way I should've handled it, but I didn't know what else to do."

"You got off the plane from where?" Holly asked.

Elima 25

"San Francisco. That's where Mario and I live. He went to work one morning, and didn't come home. I haven't seen him or heard from him in three months. He just disappeared without a trace."

Holly made some notes. "If your husband disappeared in San Francisco, why are you on Kauai?"

"Because I think he's on Kauai, Miss St. James. It's a long story . . ."

"Then I would suggest you take a deep breath, and start at the beginning."

Anna Rocettie dabbed at her eyes again before she said, "My husband owns a small art gallery in San Francisco, Miss St. James. He's also an artist. Unfortunately, he never considered 'dabbling in paints' to be anything more than a hobby, even though a lot of people thought his talent was exceptional. Two weeks ago, I received a call from a good friend who was vacationing on Kauai. He was very excited, and said he had just purchased a painting from a vendor on the beach. He said he couldn't be positive, but that it looked like Mario's work. I wanted to leave immediately, just catch the next flight to the islands, but I had obligations, and couldn't get away. And of course, there was always the chance my friend was wrong. And so, even though I finally man-

26 *Georgette Livingston*

aged to clear my calendar a few days later, I decided to wait until I could see the painting for myself.'' She took a deep, ragged breath. ''To tell you the truth, when I saw it, I almost fainted. It was even signed with an 'M'.''

Holly could feel the first stirrings of awareness, as her heart fluttered in her chest. Could Marty Ricco and Mario Rocettie be one and the same? ''Is that the way he signed his paintings?''

''No—no, he signed them 'Mario', but the 'M' looked the same, and I'd know his work anywhere!''

''Why didn't you go to the Kauai police with this?'' Holly asked.

''And get the same runaround from them that I got in San Francisco? No way. I went to the police right after Mario disappeared. They turned me over to the missing persons department, who conducted a brief—very brief—investigation. A few phone calls, that was about it. Then they listed all the reasons why a person disappears. Foul play, because a crime has been committed, embezzlement, back child support, and wanting out of a miserable marriage, to name a few. They quickly eliminated everything but a miserable marriage, and even had the nerve to suggest that that might be the reason why Mario left. Said it wouldn't be the

Elima 27

first time, nor the last. They also informed me that their computer was full of names. Missing people, unsolved cases, and that ninety percent of them didn't want to be found. I tried to tell them that Mario loved me and wouldn't walk out on me like that, but they wouldn't listen. They put me through a lot of anguish with their stupid questions, and I walked out.''

"Do you have children?" Holly asked, trying to keep her voice even.

"No kids . . . I told Mr. St. James that I'm willing to pay any amount if you'll find my husband, and I meant it."

"You'll be charged the going rate, Anna, if in fact we charge you anything at all . . . I wish there was an easier way to say this."

The woman's eyes grew round in her pale face. "You know where my husband is?"

"We don't know where he is, but there is a possibility . . . I think before we get into this—"

Anna Rocettie shook her head vigorously. "No! I want the truth! If you know where he is . . ."

Holly sighed. "Three days ago, at one of our more remote beaches, an Italian-American man, an artist with extraordinary talent, went wind surfing with friends. The friends thought the surf was too high, but the artist went out

28 *Georgette Livingston*

anyway. He didn't come back.'' Holly braced herself for the reaction. But when it came, it wasn't what she expected. No hysterics, no tears, and for a brief second, she even thought she saw anger. And then just as quickly, the woman's chin began to tremble.

"Would you like a glass of water?'' Holly asked.

"No. Did the police find the body?''

"No, but it's a big ocean out there, and the undercurrents are unpredictable. And quite frankly, the police are short on manpower. If the missing artist is your husband, he's been using the name Marty Ricco.''

That set Anna back a moment, and she scowled. "Why would he want to do that?''

"You tell me. One day he disappears in San Francisco. Three months later he turns up on Kauai using a different name. Sounds like he didn't want to be found, Mrs. Rocettie.''

Tears again, but this time, definitely in anger. "You just don't know Mario, that's all, or you wouldn't say something terrible like that.''

And maybe you don't know him, either, Holly thought, but didn't comment.

Anna Rocettie pressed on. "Besides, Mario is an excellent swimmer. When he was in his teens, he spent a lot of summers surfing in

Elima 29

Southern California, and even has ribbons and medals.''

''Accidents can still happen,'' Holly tried to reason.

''No way. Mario might be a lot of things, but he isn't stupid. He would never have gone out in the surf if he thought he couldn't handle it.''

''Providing your husband and Marty Ricco are one and the same. Fortunately, there is a way to prove it, but first things first. The police are already involved, so we'll have to bring them up-to-date.''

Anna Rocettie stood up. ''I told you what I went through in San Francisco, and it sounds like it's going to be even worse here,'' she snapped. ''I'm not hiring the police department, Miss St. James. I'm hiring St. James Investigations. If you don't want to take the case, I'll hire someone else!''

''And someone else would handle it the same way. The police have had virtually nothing to go on except the man's name. His beach friends had no idea where he lived, but one of them remembered Marty saying he was an artist, and that some of his paintings were in a local gallery. The police found the gallery, and his paintings. The gallery belongs to a friend of mine, so in a way, I was involved in this

30 *Georgette Livingston*

even before you stepped off the plane, as incredible as that sounds.''

Anna Rocettie sat down. ''And the paintings?''

''Still at the gallery. The police didn't have room to store them, so they took inventory. They also dusted for prints, hoping to come up with an address on him, which in turn, might have also helped them locate his family. But there weren't any prints on the paintings. We still haven't been able to figure that one out. In any event, you can see why it's so important for you to talk to the police. If Marty Ricco is your husband, you'll be filling in a large piece of the puzzle.''

Anna ran a shaky hand through her dark hair. ''Then I guess I don't have a choice. I'm sorry I snapped at you, but this whole thing has me a little crazy.''

Tears had filled her eyes again, and Holly managed a smile. ''I can certainly understand that. I love my husband very much, and can't imagine what it be like if he were missing.''

''You said there is a way to prove Marty Ricco is my husband?''

''Yes, or prove he isn't. You can take a look at the paintings in the art gallery, for one thing, and you can describe your husband to my

Elima 31

friend, Cindy, unless you have a photo of him.''

Anna reached in her handbag, and pulled out a snapshot. ''This was taken at Christmastime, just before he disappeared.''

She handed it to Holly, and Holly looked down at the man's smiling face. He wasn't handsome, but he was certainly attractive. Holly nodded. ''This should do it. I'll call Cindy, and tell her we're on our way. Oh, and I'll have to leave a note for my brother. Did you rent a car?''

''No, I took a cab.''

''Where are you staying?''

Anna shrugged. ''I came here right from the airport.''

Holly picked up the phone. ''I'll get you a room at the Kauai Terrace. It's a wonderful hotel, and at least you'll be comfortable.''

Twenty minutes later, Holly pulled the Blazer into a slot in front of the gift shop, and gave Anna Rocettie a comforting smile. ''I know you're nervous, but isn't finding out the truth better than not knowing at all?''

Anna gritted her teeth. ''Mario isn't dead. He *can't* be.''

Holly led the way into the gift shop, and prayed with all her heart that Anna was right.

Cindy was waiting for them near the arched

32   *Georgette Livingston*

doorway to the art gallery, and after introductions, shook hands with Anna.

"This is the snapshot of Mario Rocettie," Holly said. "What do you think?"

Cindy, looking a little frazzled, shrugged. "I don't know. This man is clean shaven and has short hair. Marty Ricco has a beard and longer hair, but he looks sort of familiar around the eyes."

Holly turned around to ask Anna if her husband had ever had long hair or a beard, but Anna was already in the art gallery, where soft lights illuminated the paintings on the wall. She was touching them, following the brush strokes with her fingers. And when she turned around, her face was awash with tears. "They are even more beautiful than the paintings he did at home," she said softly. And then she buried her face in her hands, and truly wept. Huge, convulsive sobs shook her shoulders.

Cindy went to get Anna a glass of water, while Holly tried to think of some way to comfort her, some way to tell her that everything was going to be okay. But she couldn't. Something was very, very wrong, out of kilter, and it went far beyond the fact that Mario Rocettie was missing, or possibly even dead.

Holly took a deep breath, and headed for the phone. It was time to call the police.

Chapter Three

They had dinner that night on the terrace overlooking the pool, and although Logan had tried to make it festive by lighting the tiki torches and heaping creamy white and lavender orchids in a bowl on the glass-topped table, Holly's mood was glum, and had been since she'd left Anna Rocettie at the Kauai Terrace.

She hadn't discussed it with Logan yet, other than to give him a very brief accounting, because she was trying to get it straightened out in her mind, first. And that was the problem. None of it made any sense.

"You haven't eaten much," Logan said, breaking into her thoughts.

Holly sighed. "I know, and I'll have to apol-

34   *Georgette Livingston*

ogize to Tutu, because it certainly isn't her cooking. The rack of lamb was wonderful. And you're wonderful for being so patient with me. I know I've been a wretched dinner partner, but . . .''

"Wretched is a pretty strong word, sweetheart. Preoccupied would be more like it.''

"Because my head is filled with so many puzzling, unanswered questions, it feels like a balloon filled with helium.''

"Uh-huh, I can tell. Shall I tie you down to your chair so you don't float away?''

His comment brought a smile to her face.

"That's better. Want to talk about it? Maybe I can help. For sure, it would be better than talking about my meeting that went nowhere, as usual.''

"Oh, sweetie, I'm sorry.''

Logan shrugged. "So, let's have it.''

Holly took a deep breath. "Well, like I said earlier, Mario Rocettie and Marty Ricco are one and the same, and his wife is convinced he's still alive. But I keep going back to *why* he disappeared in the first place. If they had such a good marriage like Anna says, why would he run out on her like that? And more important, if he is alive, did he deliberately set it up to make it look like a drowning? Is it a coincidence it happened the day before Anna's

Elima 35

arrival on the island? If not, and if it was staged for her benefit, how did he know she was on her way to Kauai? And the all-important question—if he really loved her, why would he want to put her through something like this?''

Logan poured coffee into her cup from the silver carafe on the table, and said, ''Did you talk to Max?''

''Yes. I called him from the gift shop, and he came right over. I didn't get a chance to talk to him alone, but after he questioned Anna, I could see he wasn't satisfied either. Oh, her answers were clear enough, and made perfect sense, and maybe that was the problem. Maybe they were too clear, too concise, like she had rehearsed the whole thing.''

''Example?''

Holly plucked an orchid out of the bowl on the table, and absently held it in her hand. ''Like when Max asked her about her relationship with her husband. She'd told me earlier that the missing persons department in San Francisco had all but alluded to the fact that a miserable marriage might be the reason for Mario's sudden, and unexplained, disappearance, and it had really upset her. It upset her even to tell me about it, and yet when Max mentioned it, she didn't blink an eye. She sim-

36 *Georgette Livingston*

ply said, 'No, that isn't possible. We had a fantastic marriage.' When he asked her if she thought her husband might have met with foul play, she said no, because Mario didn't have an enemy in the world. When he asked her if there was a chance her husband had set the whole thing up to look like a drowning, she even smiled, enumerating in great detail that her husband didn't have a wicked bone in his body, and that something 'monstrous' like that couldn't possibly have entered his kind, caring, considerate, thoughtful, loving mind, no matter what the reason. Max said, 'Not even if he was being chased by a gang of mobsters carrying guns?' She'd actually laughed at that. A high, tinkly sound that didn't sound phony at all, and said that Mario wouldn't know a mobster from a priest, and he certainly wasn't afraid of guns, because he was an excellent marksman, belonged to a gun club, and went hunting up in the California High Sierra all the time. I found that comment inane, because no matter how comfortable a person is around guns, if you have one pointed at you, you're afraid. Finally, Max asked her what *she* thought had happened to her husband, and her answer amazed me. She said she thought Mario had had an accident of some sort while he was wind surfing, had gotten 'bonked' on the head, and after the

Elima

'unpredictable' current had carried him away from the beach and his friends, he'd 'paddled' to shore, and was now walking around the streets of Kauai with a lump on his head and a case of amnesia. She told Max she was aware the Kauai police department was short on manpower, and therefore, she didn't expect them to conduct an investigation. She said she was perfectly satisfied with St. James Investigations, and that she was confident we would find her husband.''

Holly replaced the orchid in the bowl, and shook her head. ''The thing that got to me the most, Logan, was the *way* she approached the questioning. When Jack tried to question her, she was an overwrought mess, and she wasn't much better when I talked to her. And yet she seemed to be in complete control with Max.''

''Maybe it was the relief of finally coming to terms with what happened to her husband,'' Logan reasoned. ''At least in her mind. If she's convinced he's running around Kauai with a lump on his head . . .''

''And that's something else. Why would she say he 'paddled' to shore? She told me Mario wasn't stupid, that he would never have gone out in the water if he didn't think he could handle the surf, and that he was a good swimmer. She told me as a teenager, he went surfing

38 *Georgette Livingston*

in Southern California all the time, and even had ribbons and medals. And then she said he 'paddled' to shore, making it sound like he couldn't swim his way out of a wading pool. And she used *my* word. I was the one who told her about our 'unpredictable' currents, which gave me even more reason to think her answers were well thought out. And why did she make such a big deal out of telling Max she didn't want a police investigation? So she hired St. James Investigations to find her husband. Wouldn't you think she'd want all the help she can get?''

Logan was studying Holly intently, golden-brown eyes flickering over her with interest. ''You make it sound like she's the one who is up to no good, Holly.''

''I know, but I can't shake the feeling something is amiss.''

''What does Jack have to say about it?''

''Not much. He went out to get doughnuts so I could talk to Anna alone. He hadn't come back by the time we were ready to leave for the gift shop, so I left him a note, and told him to meet us there. He arrived in time for the questioning, but I don't think he paid much attention. In the interim, he'd received a call from Kim. Sara is ill, and he was in a hurry to get home.''

Elima 39

"Serious?"

"He said he thought it was the flu, and promised to call."

Logan looked at his watch. "It's almost eight. Maybe you'd better call him."

"I will, if he doesn't call by nine . . . Do you think I'm foolish to be making so much out of this?"

Logan reached across the table, and took Holly's hand. "I've never known you to be foolish, sweetheart, and your intuition is usually right on target. You haven't said, but I assume you're going to continue on with this?"

Holly nodded. "I have to, because I don't think Anna would be that comfortable around Jack, and I know he wouldn't be comfortable around her."

"So, did Anna Rocettie give you an address in San Francisco? Or the name of the art gallery?"

"No, and I didn't ask. Dumb, huh? But at that point in time, I was taking everything she said as gospel. And I believed the problem was here on Kauai, not in San Francisco."

"Did Max get that information?"

"I don't think he asked. Guess it didn't occur to him either, but I can understand that. His

40 *Georgette Livingston*

mind wasn't in San Francisco any more than mine was.''

''What about the paintings? If Mario turns up dead, they will be rightfully hers.''

Holly shook her head. ''That's one more missing piece of the puzzle. Max basically told her the same thing, but she said she didn't want them. She turned them over to Cindy, and said to donate the proceeds from any sales, less Cindy's percentage, to a charity of her choice. She said she had enough of his paintings at home. And yet earlier, when she saw the paintings for the first time, she sobbed her heart out, and said they were more beautiful than anything he had done at home. So you tell me— if she thinks her husband is still alive, why would she be so quick to get rid of his paintings?''

Logan shrugged. ''Did she come through like she promised, and offer you coffers of gold for taking the case?''

''Yes, she did, as a matter of fact. I took her to the Kauai Terrace, and got her settled in a suite. Just before I left, she handed me a blank check. I'd already told her we wouldn't charge her more than the going rate, but I don't think she heard me. Or if she did, she was still trying to make a point. 'Find my husband, and you can name your price.' ''

Elima

41

"Do you still have the check?"

"No, I wouldn't take it. I told her she'd get a bill when this is over. I know, she could take off and we won't see a penny, but the thought of carrying around a signed, blank check isn't my idea of fun."

"You could have put it in the safe in your office, or brought it home."

"But I still would've had to get from point A to B. The way my luck runs, somebody would've conked me over the head and swiped my purse."

Logan finished the coffee in his cup, and said, "Do you remember the name of the bank?"

Holly looked at the light in his eyes, and grinned. "Yes, I do, as a matter of fact. What do you have in mind?"

Logan gave her a sly wink. "I have some good friends in San Francisco, and it seems to me that's the place to start the investigation. With a little creativity, it can be done in a way that won't alert Anna Rocettie."

"Good friends, like DEA buddies?"

"Hmm, and a few friends in high places, who can open doors."

"The Bank of America on California Street."

"And were both their names on the check?"

42 *Georgette Livingston*

"Yes. Mario Rocettie, Anna Rocettie."

"But you didn't notice a home address."

"No . . . Wait, maybe Russian something."

"Russian Hill? That's a high-rent district. I'll make the calls first thing in the morning. Meanwhile, I suggest we put this on hold, and enjoy what's left of the evening. In case you haven't noticed, the moon is full."

Holly hadn't noticed, but looked up at it now, hanging low in the black velvet sky. "It's beautiful."

"Almost as beautiful as you. Ready for dessert?"

As if on cue, Tutu padded out to the terrace, carrying a bowl of strawberries and a plate of luscious, nutty-tasting cookies. And though Tutu had a smile on her face, it wasn't as bright as usual, and her voice was stern when she said, "No dinner, no dessert. If you were a *keiki, nani* Holly, that is what I would say. *Pilikia,* yeah. I can feel trouble." She scowled at Logan. "The dinner hour should be *waianapanapa*, calm, like glistening water, *kāne* Logan. Instead it is *llikai,* like the surface of the sea during a storm." She waved an arm. "Orchids, tiki torches, moonlight, and a very fine dinner, and yet you sit with you faces down to your chests."

Logan grinned. "We haven't had an argu-

Elima 43

ment, if that's what you're worried about, Tutu. *Nani* Holly has a tough case to solve, that's all.''

Tutu brightened. ''P.I. stuff, yeah, okay.''

Holly waited until Tutu had returned to the house before she said, ''I don't think Tutu cares what's going on as long as it involves P.I. stuff, or the cops. I think—''

Holly was interrupted by the phone, and she took the call. It was Jack, and his voice sounded weary. ''The doctor just left, Holly. He said Sara has the stomach flu. I thought she was dying. Oh, Holly, she was so sick.''

Holly said to Logan, ''It's the stomach flu,'' and then to Jack, ''Give her soda crackers and sips of 7-Up. That used to help me.''

''That's what the doctor said. Sorry I wasn't with it this afternoon, Holly. Where do we stand?''

Holly gave him a brief rundown, then added, ''Logan thinks we should begin the investigation in San Francisco. He has some friends there, and plans to call them in the morning. Maybe if we can get some information on the Rocetties as a couple, it will give us some answers.''

''Then you plan on following through on this?''

''As if that's a surprise?''

44 *Georgette Livingston*

Jack chuckled. "Uh-huh, well, that's what I was counting on. What about Kentaro? Are the cops going to do anything?"

"Officially, I don't think there is much they can do. They've called off the search for the body, and there weren't any signs of foul play. Case closed. Tomorrow morning, you'll read a small blurb in the paper. 'Wind-surfing accident at Anini Beach. San Francisco artist drowned in the turbulent surf.' Then they'll go on and list all the reasons why a person shouldn't wind surf, or surf, unless they know what they're doing, and enumerate all the other casualties we've had over the years."

"Unofficially?"

"I plan on talking to Max first thing in the morning. I don't think he bought Anna's story, either, and he might have some suggestions."

"Sounds good. Gotta go. Kim's calling me. Talk to you tomorrow?"

"Tomorrow, Jack. Kiss the kids, and tell Sara I hope she feels better soon. *Aloha.*"

"*Aloha au ia oe*," Jack said, and hung up.

"Do I see tears?" Logan asked, raising a brow.

Holly swallowed around the lump in her throat. "Jack just said he loves me, and he hasn't said that in a very long time."

Logan looked at his watch. "Nor have I. The

Elima 45

last time was this morning. *Aloha au ia oe,* sweetheart, and I mean that from the bottom of my heart.''

Holly was up before dawn the following morning, after spending a restless night. An unproductive night, because she still didn't have any answers. She found Tutu in the kitchen, cleaning things that were already clean, and humming a little tune.

Tutu looked up and smiled. ''I knew you would be up early, *nani* Holly. I made coffee and a breakfast cake.''

Holly shook her head. ''It's only a little after five, Tutu. What time did you get up?''

''Much before the chickens. I was restless. You were restless. I heard you. Down the hall for a glass of water three times.''

''I'm sorry, Tutu. I didn't mean to disturb you.''

''No problem. You are working on a big case. Just like Magnum, yeah. Drink some coffee, eat some cake, take a vitamin. You will feel *maika'i.*''

Holly grinned, and poured herself a cup of coffee. The little woman was definitely a wonder, and could brighten the darkest of days.

Holly was on her second piece of pineapple cake when Logan ambled in, wearing pajama

46 *Georgette Livingston*

bottoms, and a scowl on his face. "Ah-ha, that's why I couldn't find my pajama top. You're wearing it."

Holly pushed up the sleeves and shrugged. "Wearing your clothes always makes me think better."

"You were supposed to be sleeping, not thinking. What's that, pineapple cake? When did Tutu manage to make that?"

"I would venture to guess long before the rooster's first crow."

He poured a cup of coffee, and looked at the clock on the wall. "It's eight-thirty in San Francisco. I'll go to my office and make the calls now."

Holly took a cup of coffee out to the terrace to wait, and to watch the sun come up over the ridge, turning the sky lemon yellow first, and then a rich gold. Puffy clouds floated in the distance, and looked like lanterns in the sky. It was beautiful, almost celestial, and as always, it gave Holly a deep feeling of peace and contentment.

She was thinking about the first time Logan had taken her on a tour of the house and grounds, when the bell sounded, announcing the arrival of somebody at the front gate. Puzzled because of the early hour, Holly hurried

Elima 47

to the door, but Tutu was already on the intercom, arguing with the caller.

Tutu looked at Holly and scowled. "I want to know who he is, and he wants to know who I am!"

"It's Max," Max said over the intercom. "Holly, are you there?"

Holly grinned. "It's Lt. Kentaro from the police department, Tutu. Buzz him through and show him to the terrace, while I get my robe."

Tutu's frown faded. "Cops, yeah. All hours of the day and night, o' wot."

Holly giggled, and hurried down the hall. And by the time she joined Max on the terrace a few minutes later, he not only had a cup of coffee and a plate of cake in front of him, Tutu was telling him about her *keiki* on Lanai, and was calling him Max.

"Doesn't look like introductions are necessary," Holly said, giving the bear of a man a hug.

Max swallowed the cake in his mouth, and rolled his eyes in pleasure. "This lady is terrific. You're lucky you found her."

Tutu beamed, and hurried off.

"We're very lucky, and you're lucky you found us up. Must be pretty important to have you out and about this early."

Max gave her a sheepish shrug. "Well, I

48 *Georgette Livingston*

was gonna call you from the office, but I didn't want anybody listening in. As far as the department is concerned, the case of the drowned artist is closed.''

''And?''

''And I spent a miserable night thinking about it. Is Logan up?''

''He's in his office, making some calls.''

''This early?''

''San Francisco. It's nine o'clock there.''

''Anything to do with Anna Rocettie?''

''It has everything to do with Anna Rocettie. Logan has some friends in San Francisco, and thinks that's where the investigation should begin.''

''Then you didn't buy her story, either.''

''No, I didn't. Something is wrong, Max. Call it a gut feeling if you want, but there are simply too many unanswered questions.''

''And we're going to get the answers,'' Logan said, strolling across the terrace. He sat down and sighed. ''Hello, Max. I thought I heard your voice.''

''I'm not the only one who couldn't sleep last night,'' Holly said. ''Did you talk to your friends?''

''The wheels are in motion, my love. Now all we have to do is wait.''

Elima 49

Max drummed his beefy fingers on the table. "You want to fill me in on the details?"

"Sure, off the record. Anna Rocettie gave Holly a check. Holly wouldn't take it, but saw the name of the bank. Bank records should give us an address, the name of the art gallery, and financial information."

Max frowned. "I'm not following you."

"We need some background info on the Rocetties, Max, without alerting Anna Rocettie to the fact we're poking around. I learned a long time ago the less a subject knows, the better."

"You make it sound like she's guilty of something, or at least suspect."

Holly went on. "Maybe she is. What's happening here is one thing, Max, but I want to know why Mario disappeared in the first place. Think about it. He owned an art gallery. Supposedly, he had a happy marriage. He was a gifted artist, even if he only painted as a hobby, and his home was in San Francisco. So why did he disappear, only to surface on Kauai three months later, using an assumed name?"

"So maybe the marriage wasn't so happy," Max reasoned. "Maybe the wife made his life miserable, and he wanted out."

Holly said, "Then why would she make such a big deal out of trying to find him? He

50 *Georgette Livingston*

left her with everything, including the business and his paintings.''

''Maybe he cleaned out the bank account . . . Uh-huh, so if we can get that kind of information, we'll at least have a motive for her frantic search. If it's a lot of money, she might consider following him to Mars.''

''That's right,'' Logan said. ''But we can't forget she gave Holly a blank check, and made it clear St. James Investigations could fill in any amount if they find her husband.''

Max said, ''So that means there still has to be money somewhere.''

Holly nodded. ''Or there isn't any money, and the check wouldn't be worth the paper it's printed on.''

''Well, with a little luck, we'll have the answer in a few hours,'' Logan said, running a hand through his dark, tousled hair. ''Darn. I have a breakfast meeting this morning at the Sheraton Hotel. The planning commission, the mayor, and an architect from Oahu.''

''The Bali Hai project?'' Max asked.

''Yeah, and I have to be there. We had a meeting yesterday afternoon that went nowhere, and this time, I have my fingers crossed we get across the street. If the call doesn't come in before I leave, you'll have to take down the information, Holly. You'll be talking

Elima 51

to Tom, or maybe Dick. Could even be Harry.''

Holly tittered. ''Come on, Logan, are you serious?''

A dimple creased his cheek. ''Sure, I'm serious. Code names can be hilarious. I have three operatives in Los Angeles who go by Manny, Moe, and Jack.''

Max laughed heartily. ''DEA schmooze. Don't you love it?''

Holly gave Logan's hand a squeeze. ''To tell you the truth, I do. Almost as much as I love my handsome husband. Don't worry, Logan. I'll take everything down, every last detail, and I'll even have a plan by the time you get home.''

''Should be around noon.'' He winked at Max. ''And that's one of the reasons I love Holly. She's relentless.''

The call came in from ''Harry'' at ten-fifteen. Logan was still at his breakfast meeting, and Max had gone back to the office. But both were on red alert, in the event the news was spectacular. It wasn't, but it was definitely interesting, and proved what Holly had known all along. Nothing was as it seemed, and now all they had to do was figure out why.

Chapter Four

Holly had papers spread out all over the kitchen table when Logan walked in a little after noon. Tutu had all the kitchen houseplants in the sink, and was misting them with a fine spray.

Logan kissed Holly, and shook his head. "It isn't necessary to take care of the houseplants, Tutu."

Tutu clucked her tongue. "The more I do, the more time you have to keep busy, and for *nani* Holly to work on her big case. See all those papers? Look at her face. Big deal, o' wot?"

Tutu's grin was infectious, and Logan chuckled. "Yeah, it looks like a big deal to

Elima 53

me,'' he said, sitting down across from Holly. ''I take it Tom, Dick, or Harry called?''

Holly gave him a brilliant smile. ''I take it your meeting went well?''

''Nope, no way. You first.''

''Harry called. We talked for a few minutes, and then he said he was faxing me the report. Came through ten minutes later. Now, I'm trying to come up with some sort of a case file, and it isn't easy.''

Logan studied the snapshot of Mario Rocettie for a moment, and then picked up a sheet of paper. ''So the house is on Russian Hill Place.''

''That's right, an apartment house. They were renting three rooms with a view. Anna still has the apartment.''

''And the art gallery?''

''On Fisherman's Wharf. Good tourist traffic, but from the amount of money in the bank, I'd say business was slow at best. Less than six thousand, and the balance never went higher.''

''Is it a business account?''

''No. The business account is in Mario's name, and has a balance of less than five hundred dollars.''

''Makes you wonder how they could afford to rent an apartment on Russian Hill.''

54 *Georgette Livingston*

"Or how Anna could make us such a generous offer. 'Name your price' doesn't fit the pattern. What if we'd said our fee was six thousand dollars? It would have cleaned out their personal account. And something else doesn't fit. She was wearing expensive clothes and diamond earrings. And what about the airfare to the islands? Or the fact she didn't bat an eyelash when I suggested a suite at the Kauai Terrace."

Logan shook his head. "So Mario didn't clean out the bank account when he left."

"No, he didn't, and, according to the bank, there haven't been any unusually large withdrawals. It occurred to me there might be other bank accounts."

"Yeah, like in Switzerland or the Cayman Islands. How about credit cards?"

"None. You know, it amazes me that your friends could come up with so much information in a little over four hours."

Logan's eyes twinkled with amusement. "You ought to see them when it's a rush. Any background on the Rocetties before they were married?"

"Not on Anna. Harry said if we can get her fingerprints, it might help. Mario, on the other hand, worked at the art gallery as the curator for several years. When the original owner re-

Elima 55

tired, he gave Mario first chance to buy him out.''

''Maybe that's what wiped them out financially.''

''Maybe, but the price was more than reasonable, and the seller carried the paper. Mario was able to name his own terms.''

''Dates?''

Holly looked at her notes. ''They were married in March of last year, and bought the gallery in June. Mario supposedly disappeared in January, seven months later. Now it's March again, and that brings us up-to-date. It's really strange, but I got the impression they were married a lot longer than that.''

''What about Mario's family?'' Logan asked.

''No family. His parents died when he was a teenager, and he stayed with an aunt. She died five years ago. No siblings.''

''Which has to mean that Anna is the only one looking for him.''

''Hmm, and it also means we only have Anna's word regarding what happened, though she wasn't lying about contacting the police in San Francisco. No discrepancies there. The lieutenant in missing persons remembered the case. Said Anna was in his office fifteen minutes at the most. Long enough for him to

56   *Georgette Livingston*

give her a little speech about wayward husbands and how their computer was jammed with missing people. That coincides with what she told me. Except he didn't make any phone calls, like she said. He told her to wait a couple of weeks, and if her husband didn't turn up, he'd make a few phone calls, and see what he could do. She told him thanks for nothing, and stormed out. He wasn't upset, he was amused, thinking that the poor guy probably had the best reason in the world for taking off. His wife.''

Logan smiled, and Holly went on. ''And that's when the thought occurred to me. Did Anna hire a P.I. in San Francisco? It would make sense to begin the search where he disappeared, and after the falling out with the police, I can't believe she would wait three months, and only begin the search *after* a friend *happened* to buy one of his paintings on Kauai. Harry said he'd check into it, and get back to me, and I plan on asking Anna about it, too. Maybe between us, we can get a truthful answer.'' Holly looked at Logan slyly. ''By the way, Harry has a very nice voice. Is he handsome?''

Logan gave her a rakish grin. ''He's short and skinny, and has a wart on the end of his nose.''

Elima 57

Tutu tittered, but didn't comment.

Holly tittered back. "Which means he's tall, dark, and handsome, Tutu."

"Is the art gallery in both their names?" Logan went on.

"It's in Mario's name."

"What did he do before he became the gallery curator?"

"Cleaned crabs at Fisherman's Wharf, and sketched tourists for an extra buck. You know, he'd sit on a street corner and hawk his business. That's how he found out about the curator's job. Sketched the owner one day, and it went from there."

"I take it Harry talked to the original owner?"

"Yes, he did. The original owner—his name is Bert Kenny—is really upset. Anna closed the gallery right after Mario disappeared. Mr. Kenny spent years building up the gallery, and knew Mario would continue on and make it everything it should be. Then in a blink, Anna wiped it out. Mr. Kenny told Harry the building is just sitting there, empty and desolate, and it breaks his heart."

Logan scribbled a few notes on a blank piece of paper. "Have you talked to Max or Jack?"

Holly nodded. "I called them right after I

58 *Georgette Livingston*

talked to Harry. I wanted to call you, but didn't want to pull you out of your meeting.''

Logan was wearing a gray silk suit and an aloha shirt in soft blues and greens, and yanked at his tie. ''It wouldn't have mattered. The meeting was a fizzle, again. Nobody could agree on anything. Not even the building site, and it really ticks me off. If the farmers weren't dependent on our lower fifty acres, I'd suggest building the center there.''

Holly shook her head at her handsome husband whom she loved so much she could hardly stand it. ''You're wonderfully caring and giving, Logan. Tutu calls you an *aikane*, a true friend of the land, but you can only give so much. And don't they realize how important it is to have a cultural center on our island?''

''Sure they do, but they want to make sure it's economically feasible. I can understand that, the way things are today, but they aren't looking at the project over the long haul. I think before too long, I'm going to have to go to Oahu, and get a prospectus of how they handled the Polynesian Cultural Center when it was in the planning stages.''

''Hasn't that already been done?'' Holly asked.

''Sure it has, several times, but maybe they weren't asking the right questions.''

Elima 59

Tutu placed a plate of sandwiches on the only clear spot on the table, and clucked her tongue. "Even P.I.s have to eat."

Logan looked at the plate of thick turkey sandwiches, and scowled. "I thought you were misting the plants. When did you do that?"

"You talk, I work. Now eat. Hot tea or iced tea?"

"Hot tea sounds lovely, Tutu, and thanks. Don't let *kāne* Logan's scowl disturb you. He appreciates you as much as I do," Holly assured her.

Tutu grinned, and padded off.

Logan took a healthy bite of sandwich, and shook his head. "I've said it before, and I'll say it again. That woman is a marvel. Now, where were we? Okay, Max and Jack. What did they say?"

"Not much, but they were both amazed we got the info so quickly from San Francisco. Jack said Anna has called three times today to see how the investigation is going. He said she sounded fidgety, out of sorts, and very impatient."

"Thank goodness she doesn't have our home phone number," Logan said.

"Amen. Jack also said Sara is feeling better, and it's a good thing, because he just got another case. Insurance fraud. This one is big

60 *Georgette Livingston*

time, involving a lot of money. Jack is really good at that sort of thing, so I told him to concentrate on that, and we'll handle Anna Rocettie.''

''And Max?''

''He said I would be the best candidate to get Anna's fingerprints, and of course I agreed. I plan to pay her a visit later this afternoon, and go from there. I haven't anything to report, so I'll have to come up with some reason for dropping in on her unannounced, but you know me. I'll think of something.''

''Unannounced, huh?''

Holly grinned. ''Isn't that the only way? So, my gorgeous, handsome husband, if Harry happens to call while I'm gone, *you'll* have to talk to him.''

''What if I'm out in the garden, pulling weeds?''

''Tutu can call you in from the garden.''

''What if I'm down in the cane fields, talking to a farmer?''

''Then Tutu can take the call. I'll bet she'd get a kick out of talking to 'Operative Harry,' and listening to his husky voice. Bet she'd get everything down, too, including the commas and periods.''

Logan grinned. ''So, when are you going?''

Elima 61

"Just as soon as I can finish putting this file together."

Logan reached across the table, and squeezed Holly's hand. "Be careful?"

"I'll be careful."

"Have you figured out how you're going to get Anna's fingerprints?"

"Hopefully from a drinking glass. I'll work out the details on the way to the hotel."

"If you run into Nikko Von Sant, give him my best."

"I will. I didn't see him when I took Anna to the hotel, but I did talk to him on the phone when I arranged for the suite. He's doing very well, and plans on remodeling the south tower."

"He always seems to be remodeling something."

"Yes, but you know Nick. It's his hotel, and he wants it to be the best it can be. He might be a paraplegic, but he has more courage and determination than twenty men."

"Sounds like somebody else I know," Logan said, giving Holly a sultry wink. "Like Jack always says, 'Go get 'em, tiger.' "

It was almost four o'clock when Holly made her way up to the seventh floor of the Kauai Terrace. She'd stopped at the office to see Nick

62　*Georgette Livingston*

first, and explain the circumstances, and it had been his suggestion she take along an extra glass to replace the one she planned to swipe. ''Can't leave any loose ends.'' He'd grinned with enthusiasm, adding, ''Boy, do I love all this P.I. stuff. If I wasn't in the hotel business, I'd be on your doorstep, asking for a job.''

Holly smiled, thinking about Nick rolling around in his wheelchair doing undercover work, and how good he would be. She knocked on the door to Anna's suite.

Nothing. She knocked again, louder this time, and then pounded. It hadn't occurred to her the woman might be out, and she was about to give up when the door opened.

Anna Rocettie looked flushed and mussed, and tightened the belt on her dark-green satin robe. ''Oh, it's you!'' she exclaimed, with her cupid's-bow mouth forming a perfect circle. ''I-I was taking a nap . . .''

Holly planted a smile on her face, and said, ''I had some business in the hotel, and thought I'd stop by and see how you're doing. My brother said you'd called.''

Anna Rocettie sighed, and ran a hand through her tangled hair. ''I've called your office several times, actually, and to tell you the truth, I got the distinct feeling your brother was giving me the runaround.''

Elima 63

Holly had to mentally glue on the smile, and said, "My brother is a very busy man, Anna, and he's doing everything he can. Something like this takes time. And you have to understand, we do have other cases. By the way, did you hire a P.I. in San Francisco?"

"No. No, I didn't. It didn't occur to me. I guess I wasn't thinking, but then, I was *so* upset. I couldn't even function for weeks."

"But you went to the police."

"Only because I thought something might have happened to him," Anna said a little breathlessly. "San Francisco is a wonderful city, but like all big cities, it has its share of unsavory characters. Anything can happen."

They were still standing in the doorway, and it was apparent Anna wasn't going to invite Holly in. No entry, no glass with fingerprints, Holly thought, and swept into the room, brushing by Anna with ease. She waved an arm. "How do you like your suite? Are you comfortable?"

Anna closed the door, a bit reluctantly, Holly thought, and grimaced. "It will do."

Holly looked around at the plush white furniture, cane accents, and vases of exotic flowers, and had the feeling Anna Rocettie considered this slumming. There were two rooms, the sitting room and the bedroom. The

64 *Georgette Livingston*

bedroom door was closed, but the balcony door was open to the soft sea breeze. And there was something else. Perfume? Maybe, or maybe it was only the scent of the flowers. It was familiar, but Holly couldn't place it.

Holly looked at Anna thoughtfully, after visually inspecting the portable bar in the corner. Six glasses on the small, attached counter. Four still wrapped in paper, two used. "You really look out of it, Anna, and I'm so terribly sorry. I know you are under a great deal of stress. Tell you what. Put some clothes on, and I'll take you out for a bite to eat."

Anna was shaking her head. "I planned to call room service . . ."

"Nonsense! The prices are outrageous, and you need to get out of here, if only for an hour or so. You can't spend all your time cooped up. Besides, it will give us a chance to have a little chat."

"We can chat here."

"And we can chat somewhere else. We don't have to leave the hotel. There are some really nice restaurants downstairs, or we can go to the coffee shop . . . I know, we'll go to the Surf Room. It's a wonderful lounge with big, comfy booths, and they serve snacks. Perfect. Now run along and get dressed. I won't take no for an answer!"

Elima 65

Holly held her breath, but the woman finally nodded. "I'll only be a minute," she muttered, and headed for the bedroom.

The second the door closed behind Anna, Holly hurried to the bar. She smelled both glasses, decided they had contained only water, and made the switch, wrapping the used glass in a handkerchief. With the glass tucked safely in her tote, she sat down in a chair and waited.

A few minutes later, Anna came out of the bedroom, still wearing her robe. She shook head. "I-I'm sorry, but we'll have to do this some other time. I'm not feeling well. Must be the humidity, but I feel light-headed, and nauseous."

Holly feigned concern, though what she *really* felt was relief. "Oh, dear. I'm so sorry. Well, you take care of yourself, you hear? I'll call you tomorrow, and see how you're doing. *Aloha.*"

Holly hurried out, and when she was in the hall, she took a deep breath. The *last* thing she wanted was to spend an hour or so with Anna Rocettie, making idle chatter while her mind was on fast-forward. She'd finally placed the scent wafting around the room, for one thing, and it wasn't perfume or the flowers. It was a man's fragrance, and one she should be familiar with, because Logan had a bottle of it sit-

66 *Georgette Livingston*

ting on his dresser. He didn't wear it because she didn't care for it, but it was very expensive, and memorable. Had Anna been entertaining a man in the bedroom? Was that why she'd looked so flushed and rumpled? But with that thought came another. Had the man used one of the glasses? If so, did she have the right one?

Holly shook her head, and punched the elevator button. She'd handled it all wrong. She should have asked for a drink of water *before* suggesting they go out to eat, and then made the switch, thus assuring Anna's fingerprints would be on the glass.

The thought that she might have to do this all over again aggravated her, and put a scowl on her face.

Holly found Logan barbecuing chicken on the terrace. She kicked off her sandals. She raised her face for his kiss, but had a hard time with a smile. "Where is Tutu?"

"I explained how much I enjoy barbecuing, and gave her the night off. I thought she'd go see her sister or something, but she's in her room, watching TV."

"Has she eaten?"

"No, but I promised her I'd take her a plate. She feels funny about eating with us, sweet-

Elima 67

heart, so I think we'd better respect how she feels. Maybe later on, after she's been here a while, she'll feel differently. So, did you get the glass?''

''I did, but it might be the wrong glass.'' She explained what had happened, and sighed. ''Unfortunately, it didn't occur to me until I was out in the hall.''

Logan shrugged. ''If it is, you'll have to work out another plan. You're creative, sweetheart. Why the long face?''

''Because if it is the wrong glass, I've wasted a lot of time. And I'm angry with myself. I should have picked up on the cologne right away. I should have realized she'd had a man in her suite, and that he might have handled one of the glasses.''

''And then what? You would've had to make other plans anyway, so what's the difference?''

''Yes, but I could have saved us all a lot of time if I'd been thinking on my feet.''

''Could have, should have, would have, might have. Come on, Holly. You're making too much of it. And I'll tell you something else. If Tutu sees that frown on your face, she's going to have a fit.'' He pushed a chair close to her. ''Put your feet up, and I'll get you something to drink.''

68   *Georgette Livingston*

A few minutes later, Logan returned with two iced glasses and a filled pitcher. He gave her another kiss, and grinned. "That's better. At least the frown is gone."

Holly took a sip of her cool drink, and reached into her tote. "Well, at least I did something right. Here's the glass. I only touched the bottom."

"Leave it on the table for now, Holly. It's going to take some time to lift the latents and fax them to San Francisco, and dinner comes first."

"As it should," Holly said, beginning to relax. "I think the one thing that upsets me the most is that woman. What kind of a game is she playing? How can she be a grieving, hysterical wife one day, and entertain a man the next? I saw no signs of tears today, either, and I got the distinct feeling she loathes the suite. Makes me wonder what she's accustomed to. Did Harry call?"

"He did. Anna wasn't lying to you. She didn't hire a P.I. in San Francisco."

"So the question is, why didn't she? I don't buy the fact that it didn't occur to her, or that she was *so* upset, she couldn't function for weeks. She had enough wits about her to go to the police."

Elima 69

Logan brushed barbecue sauce on the chicken. "You want to hear a little theory?"

"I'm all ears."

"Okay. Mario Rocettie cleaned crabs and sketched tourists for a living, which leads me to believe life was one big struggle. And then he got a job at the art gallery. A step up, but hardly enough to make him wealthy. So, he met Anna and married her. What if Anna had a lot of money, and he got greedy? What if he took off with her jewelry, or something else of value? Something worth enough to give him a fresh start in life."

Holly shook her head. "You're not describing the beach bum who was willing to take peanuts for his paintings, Logan."

"What if he couldn't sell what he took from Anna right away? What if he decided to wait until the heat was off? He'd have to survive in the meantime. What better way than to lose himself on an island, and turn a little hobby into something that would bring in some money? So, he changes his name, and settles down, doing what he does best. And then fate steps in by way of one of Anna's friends, who just happens to be on Kauai, and buys one of his paintings, and sets this whole unbelievable affair in motion."

Holly was shaking her head again. "So how

did Mario know his wife was coming to the island?''

''That's a big question, Holly, and I haven't the foggiest, but like everything else, there is an answer.''

''That also makes Mario the bad guy.''

''Maybe he is.''

''But that would also make him very, very stupid,'' Holly reasoned. ''He gives his work under his assumed name to vendors on the beach to sell, and puts his work in an art gallery, knowing tourists love that kind of stuff. Tourists might come from all over the world, Logan, but they also come from the mainland. Would he chance putting his work on display like that?''

Logan said, ''He might when you consider the odds of one of his paintings getting back to his wife. A million to one, sweetheart, and I'll bet he thought it was worth taking the chance. Especially if he was desperate for money.''

''He could have gotten a regular job,'' Holly went on, feeling a sudden need to defend the man, yet knowing everything Logan was saying made perfect sense.

''No way. He would've had to give out a Social Security number, for one thing, and an address.''

Elima 71

They were going around in circles, getting nowhere, and Holly had a headache. "Well, I know one thing for sure," she said finally. "You might think Mario is the bad guy, but I don't trust Anna Rocettie. And there is a lot more to this than meets the eye."

Logan stepped behind her, and wrapped his arms around her. "I know, my love, and it's cases like this that can drive a person crazy. You're tense. How does that feel?"

Logan was massaging her shoulder muscles, and Holly closed her eyes. It felt wonderful. And Logan was wonderful, reminding her that no case, no matter how exasperating, could take away the magic they shared. She loved him with all her heart, forever and ever, and even after that.

It was after midnight when Logan finally came to bed. Holly opened her arms to him, and he gathered her close.

As soon as he'd gone to the wine cellar after dinner to work on the fingerprints, she'd gone to bed. But even though she was exhausted, she wasn't able to sleep. Twice she'd gone to the kitchen for a glass of water, and the last time, she'd bumped into Tutu in the hall. "Warm milk," Tutu said, after taking one look at Holly's face. Holly had let the dear little

72 *Georgette Livingston*

woman bring her a glass of warm milk, but that hadn't helped, either. Nothing would until all the puzzle pieces were in place.

Nothing but Logan's love, Holly thought now, raising her face for his sweet kisses.

"I faxed the latents to San Francisco," Logan said, between kisses. "Now all we have to do is wait."

"All we have to do is wait," Holly repeated, snuggling close.

Chapter Five

Holly looked out at the soft, romantic lighting flickering across the lagoon, and took a deep breath of enjoyment. Tutu had insisted they go out to dinner, and Logan had suggested the Coco Palms Hotel. Now they were standing on the footbridge near the exotic Flame Room, having drinks while they waited for a table overlooking the lagoon, and it truly was a wonderful spot to unwind.

They had arrived just in time to see the Torchlight Ceremony, which had been a nightly tradition at the Coco Palms for years. And although Holly had seen it many times, she still got a thrill out of listening to the sounds of the drums and blowing conch shells

74 *Georgette Livingston*

as scantily clothed islanders ran among the palm trees and then snaked along the lagoon, leaving a trail of lighted torches. Everyone watching the ceremony felt a little breathless.

It had been a tedious day at best, waiting for the fax from San Francisco, and it hadn't helped when Jack called to say that Anna Rocettie was driving him crazy. "Call her!" he'd exclaimed. "And get her off my back!"

Reluctantly, Holly made the call, and Anna's response had been unbelievable. "I don't want to hear what *isn't* going on, Miss St. James. It's a waste of my time and yours. Just find my husband!"

Holly tried to reason with her, but couldn't keep the snip out of her voice when she said, "You've been calling the office, Anna, and that's wasting my brother's time."

Anna snapped back, "Well, I certainly can't call you. You're never in the office!"

"When I'm working on a case, it doesn't have to revolve around the office," Holly returned. "And you know the old saying—don't call us, we'll call you. Try to relax, Anna. We're doing everything we can."

Anna had uttered an expletive before slamming down the phone, and Holly had wanted to scream.

Max had called, too, just to check in, and

Elima 75

then Logan had gotten into an argument on the phone with Bob Dolan, because the man wanted to rehash the upheaval they'd had at the breakfast meeting, and Logan wanted to keep the line clear. Tutu did her best to keep the mood light, but found it a formidable task.

Finally, a little after five o'clock, Tutu had pulled Holly aside, and said, "This is no good, *nani* Holly. Sour faces and short tempers. Go out to dinner. Candlelight, soft music. *Kāne* Logan in a white jacket, and you in a beautiful *holomu* with flowers in your hair, yeah. Hold hands, and forget what awaits you here." When Holly had reminded Tutu they were waiting for an important fax, Tutu had rolled her eyes, and said, "Give me the number where you go, and when the paper rolls out of that thing, I'll call."

"Sorry we came?" Logan asked, interrupting Holly's thoughts.

"Mmm, I'm glad we came. When Jack and I were kids, Dad always brought us here on my birthday. When it was Jack's birthday, he'd pick the fancy hotel luaus because of all the food, but I wanted to come here because I loved the Torchlight Ceremony, and all the little thatched-roof honeymoon cottages nestled on the other side of the lagoon. I'd wonder what they looked like inside, and dream of

76 *Georgette Livingston*

staying in one of them someday with my new husband, and strolling hand in hand along the winding pathways bordering the lagoon.''

Logan groaned. ''You should've said something, sweetheart. We could have spent our honeymoon here instead of going to Maui.''

Holly grinned up at him. ''What, and miss meeting Stump Tanner, and all that adventure and excitement? We had a wonderful honeymoon, my love, in spite of everything that happened. I'd love to go back again, one of these days, because I'm head over heels in love with that old pirate.''

''Well, he's sure in love with you,'' Logan said with a twinkle in his eye. ''And it sounds like fun. Maybe this time, we could sail over. We have an anniversary coming up in a couple of months. Maybe we could do it then. Lots of room on the yacht. We could take Tutu, and our friends, and make it a party. A first anniversary to remember.''

Holly tittered. ''If we took all our friends, the boat would sink.''

''But we wouldn't be able to take all our friends, even if I chartered a cruise ship. It will take a good twelve hours over and back, running at a normal speed, and we'd want to stay a day or two. Not everybody could get away for that length of time.''

Elima 77

Holly took a sip of her drink. "Okay, then let's list all our friends who might be able to get away, and who aren't prone to seasickness, and go from there."

For the next few minutes, they worked on a verbal list, and ended up with three couples for a total of nine people, including themselves and Tutu. And it felt wonderful to be discussing pleasant things, instead of the case.

"I'd like to include Buzzy and his daughter, if they're here," Holly said a little wistfully.

Logan chuckled. "What would a trip like that be without Buzzy Caghorn?" His voice softened. "I know you miss him, sweetheart, and so do I. He's a good friend, and you've been through a lot together, but he'll be back in June, as soon as school is out on the mainland. And although we could certainly postpone the trip to include them, I doubt that Buzzy would want to take off again so soon, for whatever reason. It's going to take some time getting his daughter settled in, and things on an even keel, and he has his job to consider."

"You're right, and I know he's only been gone a few weeks, but I haven't heard from him, and I keep thinking, what if his ex-wife changes her mind, and decides she *doesn't* want to marry that guy, and refuses to give

78 *Georgette Livingston*

Buzzy custody? I know Buzzy has said all along as soon as he's a cop and can show the court he's stable and financially capable of taking care of his daughter, he's going to fight for custody, but this would be so much easier. And a lot easier on Alex, too. She's only seven, Logan, and that's such a vulnerable age. As it is, Buzzy is concerned about how this is going to affect her.''

Logan gave Holly a hug. ''Are you thinking about yourself at that age?''

''Yes, I am, as a matter of fact. I was eight when my mother died, and it was devastating. But at least I knew my mother loved me. But to walk out on your child . . . Oh, Logan, how can she do that?''

''Maybe she felt Alex would be better off with her father under the circumstances,'' Logan reasoned. ''Supposedly the man she's marrying hates kids, and that would be a pretty miserable existence.''

Holly thought back to the days when she and Buzzy were kids, living in the same neighborhood and going to the same school in the Nawiliwili district of Kauai. She was the only kid far and wide who hadn't been afraid of him, or in awe of him because of his massive size. He'd been a bully then, but she'd understood. Being a bully made it easier to cope with the

Elima 79

loneliness that was bound to come when a kid was "different."

Holly had lost touch with Buzzy after high school, and then one day, there he was, standing in the office, grinning from ear to ear, ready to pick up their friendship. And what a friendship it was.

Buzzy had gone to live with his father on the mainland after high school, and marriage, a daughter, and a bitter divorce followed. But it wasn't until his mother died and left him the little house in Nawiliwili that he realized this was where he belonged.

Holly and Logan had only been home from their honeymoon a week or so when Buzzy walked in that day unexpectedly, and the timing couldn't have been better, because her life was in danger. Logan, who had liked Buzzy immediately, hired him to be her bodyguard and, from there, they had been thrown into an incredible adventure, a near-death situation, and Buzzy had literally saved her life. It wasn't long after that Logan had gotten Buzzy a job as a bouncer at a well-known club on the southern tip of the island, but it was only a temporary arrangement, because Buzzy planned on being a cop. He'd sworn off gumdrops—his passion and Holly's ever since they were kids—had lost weight, and was studying

80 *Georgette Livingston*

hard to pass the law enforcement test coming up in October. And Logan believed, as she did, that he would be a valuable asset to the department.

Holly touched the amethyst and crystal bracelet Buzzy had given her last Christmas, and felt tears sting her eyes. He'd had the purple stones cut to simulate gumdrops, knowing that purple had been her favorite flavor, and it had been a gift that had touched her heart. It had been a Christmas full of wonderful gifts, and love, and plans. . . .

"No tears tonight," Logan said, kissing Holly's cheek. "Buzzy deserves a solid round of happiness here, and he'll get it. You'll see. And then we'll have a party, welcoming Alex to our island, and then we'll have another party when Buzzy passes the test. And then we'll have a party when he graduates from the academy, and another party, just to celebrate life in general, because we all have so much to be thankful for. Are you worn out yet?"

Holly looked up at Logan's smiling face with stars in her eyes, and had never loved him more.

They had finished a fabulous lobster dinner, and were drinking one last cup of coffee, when the waiter came to their table to tell Logan he

Elima 81

had a phone call, and that he could take it at the hostess station. Holly held her breath while Logan made his way to the podium-type structure near the open, airy entrance, and then she felt her heartbeat accelerate as she watched the expression on his face. Without a doubt, the fax had come in from San Francisco, and their wonderful evening was over.

Holly was standing beside Logan when he hung up the phone. "Is this it?" she asked.

"This is it, my love. Let's go home."

Twenty minutes later, Holly and Logan walked into the house, and were met with Tutu's animated theatrics—frowns, scowls, and flailing arms. "P.I. stuff, cop stuff, okay. Paper running out of that thing, okay, yeah. But the telephone calls! First *nani* Holly's brother, then Max, then Cindy Tolover, then somebody named Buzzy. What kind of name is that!"

After Logan headed for the office, Holly managed to get in, "Buzzy Caghorn is a dear friend, Tutu. Did he leave a message?"

Tutu nodded. "Said he is home."

Torn between happiness because Buzzy was home, and worry, for the very same reason, Holly said, "Did he mention his daughter?"

"No, no daughter."

Concerned for her friend, wondering if he'd come home ahead of schedule because his ex-

82 *Georgette Livingston*

wife had changed her mind, Holly shook her head, and tried to concentrate on the moment. They had the fax, and now maybe they would have some answers.

But when she walked into the office and saw Logan's scowling face, she groaned. "Uh-oh, what's wrong?"

Logan was sitting at his desk holding the fax, and his sigh was heartfelt. "We seem to be in the middle of something a lot bigger than we thought, my love. The fingerprints weren't Anna's. They belong to Frank Denado, big-time racketeer and professional thief, who has been one step ahead of the law for as long as I can remember. Here's his photo, and a photo of his current lady friend, one Analisa Newfall. We know her as Anna Rocettie."

Holly sucked in her breath, and looked at the photos. The female's hair was a little shorter, and she looked like she had been partying for a week, but it was definitely Anna Rocettie. Frank Denado resembled Jack Palance on a bad day. Holly shuddered.

Logan said, "Did we get a last name on Anna before she married Mario?"

"I'm not sure . . ." Holly went over to the side table where she'd put her notes, and shuffled through the stack of papers. "Uh-huh, here it is. Brown. Anna Lee Brown. She gave a

Elima 83

downtown San Francisco hotel as her address when they took out the marriage license in Lake Tahoe. That's where they were married. No wait, no fuss. The hotel in San Francisco didn't have anything on her, and that's when Harry ran into his dead end.''

''What about the bank? You can't open an account without giving them a little information.''

''Same thing. The joint account was opened in October, three months before Mario disappeared. She listed her mother's maiden name as Thomas, said she didn't have her Social Security card with her, but that she would call in the number. She never did, and the bank never followed up on it. Or maybe they just hadn't gotten around to it. I don't believe any of this, Logan. If the fingerprints on the glass belong to Frank Denado, then that means he's the man Anna had in her suite. It was *his* cologne I smelled, and he's in the middle of this mess, too. But why?''

''Better yet, how does he fit in?'' Logan said, running a hand through his hair. ''Denado has been on the wanted list for years, but he's a very creative man. Some might even consider him a genius. And everybody wants him. CIA, AFT, DEA, FBI, even Interpol. Unfortunately,

84 *Georgette Livingston*

his inventiveness is what's kept him a free man.''

Holly sat down in the chair beside Logan's desk, and held her head in her hands. ''Wonderful. So, when do we call in the troops?''

Logan handed her another fax. ''As soon as possible. This came in just before we got home.''

Holly looked at the fax, and shook her head. It was from Harry, and the wheels were already in motion. The interested agencies were being notified, but because of jurisdiction, and the fact that Frank Denado was thought to be dealing in drugs at the present time, Logan and his DEA buddies had top priority. ''Bet that's going to upset a few people,'' she said finally.

''To say the least. I'm not going to wait until morning to make the calls, Holly. I'll do it tonight. This is too important, and we'll need all available hands on board.''

Holly was looking at the first fax now, which was more like a dossier, and couldn't believe what she was reading. Nothing much on Anna, except that she had been Denado's lady friend for several years, and was thought to be an accomplice. But the skinny on Frank Denado was an entirely different matter. Although he had had his hands in just about every criminal activity known to man at one time or

Elima 85

another, drugs and gun smuggling seemed to be his favorite enterprises. But not to be overlooked was his penchant for thievery. He was thought to be the mastermind in several jewelry heists, involving millions of dollars, and he wasn't opposed to stealing artwork, either. Most of the interested agencies believed he was the man responsible for the disappearance of a priceless painting out of a Paris art gallery, but that had been two years ago, and nobody had any proof. Frank Denado was also known as the "king of the alibis" and, unfortunately, his alibis always held up.

"The thing that jerks my chain the most," Logan said, "is the fact that this guy has never done time. Not even a nickel. Not even when he was a punk kid in Chicago, robbing everybody blind. They'd haul him in, and let him go, because they never had enough evidence to hold him. He moved from Chicago to New York, then to San Francisco, and then to Europe. It wasn't long before the world was his playground."

"Oh, Logan, and *we're* supposed to catch him?"

Logan picked up the phone, and punched in a number. Within minutes, he was talking to Rob Miller on Oahu.

Holly left the office, feeling dejected and

86 *Georgette Livingston*

weary, and very much aware of what was going to happen next.

She found Tutu sitting at the kitchen table, drinking a cup of tea, and sat down across from her. "I know this has been an exhausting evening for you, Tutu, but I thought I'd better tell you it's going to get worse before it gets better. We are about to become overrun with cops. Right now, *kāne* Logan is talking to one of his DEA buddies on Oahu, so it's only a matter of time. The case we've been working on has turned out to be a very big deal. I'm not going to try to explain it to you, but I wanted you to know what to expect."

Tutu grinned. "The Feds, like Eliot Ness, o' wot?"

Holly couldn't help but smile. "Just about. Fortunately, *kāne* Logan's agency has jurisdiction, so the investigation will be limited to DEA. I have no idea what kind of a part I'm going to play in this, if any, but we will still need to make some preparations. I don't expect you to help out, but . . ."

"Help? How?" Tutu asked, with her eyes very bright.

"Well, for one thing, DEA agents are always hungry. Sandwiches will do, and it will keep them from raiding the refrigerator. They'll spend a good deal of their time trying

Elima 87

to come up with a viable plan, so they drink lots of coffee to stay awake. Oh, and they have a sweet tooth, too, big enough to fill the Kilauea Crater. I know we have some cookies in the freezer . . .''

Out came the pans, flour and sugar, and various other ingredients for cookies, while Tutu addressed what else had to be done. Last but not least, she was going to air out the bedding that was stored in the closet, even though Holly told her the men probably wouldn't sleep a wink. It didn't matter. It was best to be prepared. Tutu was going to help in every way she could, and simply oozed adrenaline.

Knowing better than to argue with her, Holly hauled out the large coffee urn, filled it with water, and measured the correct amount of coffee. Tutu's eyes bulged when she realized what Holly was doing, and shook her head. ''I thought that was for parties,'' she said simply, and went back to the cookies.

''DEA powwow parties,'' Holly said, beginning to feel the excitement herself. Max had called it DEA schmooze, but it was more than that. It was a way of life, the good guys after the bad guys, and there wasn't another feeling quite like it in the world.

While Holly waited for the coffee, she sliced roast beef and ham, made room in the refrig-

88 *Georgette Livingston*

erator for the heaping plates, and listened to Tutu sing. The little lady wasn't only a gem, she was an island treasure.

When the coffee was ready, Holly took a cup in to Logan. He was off the phone, sorting through her notes, while compiling his own. "So what's the plan?" she asked, sitting on the edge of the desk.

Logan rubbed his eyes with his fingers. "Well, for one thing, it's going to be a long night. We've decided to keep things down to a minimum at first. You know the old adage about too many chiefs and not enough Indians. Eddie Johnson is on his way to Oahu to pick Rob up in the helicopter. Ty Anderson is picking up Bill Cooper in his car, and they should be here within the hour."

"Ty Anderson . . . Oh, that nice African-American agent who took me to the safe house that night that seems like a million years ago."

"That's right, sweetheart. Wow, it does seem like years ago. He retired right after that incident, but I had the feeling this would bring the operatives out of the woodwork. The rest of the agents who are available will be on call. By the time everybody is filled in, somebody might come up with a feasible plan to nail this crook, once and for all.

Elima 89

"Did you tell Tutu what's about to happen?"

"Yes, I did. I didn't go into details, but she knows the case we've been working on has taken an important twist, and we're about to be overrun with cops. Did you call Max?"

"I did. He can't neglect his job for this, but he wants us to keep him posted. You'll have to call Jack and Cindy . . ."

"I'll call them in the morning," Holly said. "No point in everybody on the island losing sleep."

"Did I hear Tutu say Buzzy called?"

Holly nodded. "He's home. I want to call him, but I'm dragging my feet. I'm scared to death it's bad news. He didn't say anything to Tutu about his daughter, and that could mean my fears have been realized, and his ex-wife changed her mind."

Logan handed Holly the phone. "Call him, Holly. You'll feel better knowing, one way or the other."

"And if he didn't bring Alex home?"

"Then my heart goes out to him. I'll leave the rest up to you."

"The rest, like maybe you'd like to have his help on the case?"

Logan nodded. "I won't deny it. Buzzy has

90 *Georgette Livingston*

a good head for this kind of thing, and that's why he's going to make a fine cop.''

Holly punched in Buzzy's number, and he answered on the first ring. Trying to swallow around the lump in her throat, she said, ''*Aloha*, my friend. I'm tickled you're home safe and sound, but—''

Buzzy interrupted with a sigh. ''The ex changed her mind, Holly. She decided she didn't want to marry the guy. Ain't that a crock? It wasn't a wasted trip, 'cause I got to see Alex, but darn that woman. Don't think there is a more aggravating woman in the world.''

Holly looked at Logan, and shook her head. ''How did Alex take it?''

''Like a little champ. She's tough, and she can roll with the punches. Takes after me. I gave the ex fair warning. Told her that as soon as I have things together here, I'm gonna hire a lawyer, and fight for custody. I also told her Alex is spending Christmas vacation with me. Period. No ifs, ands, or buts. 'Nuff about me. What's going on? Something is. I can hear it in your voice. Right, don't tell me. You've got yourself in another mess.''

''A big mess, Buzzy, and Logan is right in it with me. I don't want to go into it on the phone . . .''

Elima 91

"Uh-huh, so just answer me this: do you want my help?"

"Major big-time. Logan and I both have our fingers crossed you'll consider it."

"Uh-huh. So, is this it-can-wait-until-morning? Or shall I drive up now?"

"Now, Buzzy, if you don't mind."

"Mind? Heck, no. Gotta tell ya, as much as I enjoyed being with my daughter, I missed this kind of stuff. Whoa. I'm gone three weeks, and look what happens. I'm on my way."

Holly hung up, and looked at Logan. "He's on his way."

Clearly pleased, Logan nodded, then grinned. "Better tell Tutu to cook a turkey. The biggest one we have in the freezer."

Chapter Six

Holly was in the kitchen putting coffee cups on a tray when the helicopter stormed overhead, circled twice, and then came in for a landing. A few minutes later, Bill "Coop" Cooper came up from the wine cellar, where Logan had his state-of-the-art surveillance equipment, and hurried out the terrace door to meet Rob at the landing pad.

Clearly excited by what was going on, Tutu added a plate of butter cookies to the tray, listened to the rotary blades slapping the air, and said, "This Rob Miller. Is he big like the others?"

Holly smiled. "Rob is short and stocky, Tutu, but he's a very nice-looking man. He

Elima   93

lives on Oahu with his beautiful wife, Julie, and is one of *kāne* Logan's best friends.''

''That man, Coop, is short, too, but very, very wide. And the handsome black man is as tall as a palm tree.'' She rolled her eyes. ''*Kāne* Logan is a very large man, but that man called Buzzy. He is a giant!''

''Buzzy also has a heart as big as the moon,'' Holly said, filling a carafe with coffee. ''And so do you, Tutu. You've been a tremendous help, but it's getting late. Why don't you go to bed?''

Tutu shook her head. ''I will sleep. I will get more sleep than you this night, *nani* Holly, but there are still things to be done, yeah.''

Knowing better than to argue with the rotund little woman, Holly gave her a hug, and carried the tray down the stairs to the cellar.

While Ty and Buzzy helped themselves to coffee and cookies, Logan tacked a large sheet of paper to the bulletin board on the wall across from the wine racks, and adjusted the lighting so it was the focal point in the room. Holly knew from experience the sheet of paper would eventually become a blueprint of their ideas and thoughts, thrown into a collage at first, but eventually taking the shape of a master plan.

Logan took a black marker and wrote two

94 *Georgette Livingston*

names at the top of the paper: Anna Rocettie, aka Analisa Newfall, and Frank Denado. He had also made copies of the photos, including the snapshot of Mario.

Holly sat down at the wooden table next to Buzzy, and gave his hand a squeeze. "I'm truly sorry things didn't work out for you, Buzzy, but I'm glad you're here. My little case has turned into a major event."

Ty Anderson chuckled. "And that's what you get for marrying Logan, pretty lady. Trouble seems to follow him around."

Ty was a tall African-American man with gray hair and a warm smile, and had a deep, mesmerizing voice.

"The same thing could be said for Holly," Logan replied, giving Holly a wink.

A few minutes later, Rob and Coop walked down the stairs and, after handshakes and hugs, the meeting was under way.

Logan gave the men a thorough accounting, then said, "So you see what we're up against. It's a scenario that could go in a dozen different directions, but the fact remains, Denado is on the island, and we have to find out what he's up to. And not to be overlooked is the fact Anna Rocettie is really Analisa Newfall, who has supposedly been involved with Denado for several years."

Elima 95

"So where does Mario Rocettie fit in?" Rob asked.

"Maybe he was an accomplice, too," Ty suggested. "Maybe he double-crossed them somehow, and they're out for blood."

"Or maybe they were using him," Holly said thoughtfully. "And when he found out about it, he ran."

For the next hour, they discussed every possible motive they could think of for the two culprits to be on the island, and why Mario disappeared in the first place, until every inch of the paper on the wall had been filled with Logan's heavy scrawl. They were left not only with a hodgepodge collage, but dozens of unanswered questions.

It also left Holly with the gut feeling that Mario's life was in danger. Finally, she said, "I think the reason Mario disappeared on the mainland is the same reason he disappeared here. He was, and is, afraid for his life. I think Anna hired St. James Investigations because she thought it was the easiest and quickest way to find her husband. And I also think they plan to kill him. I don't think she wanted the cops involved, because she simply didn't want to become involved with cops, for obvious reasons."

96   *Georgette Livingston*

"Then why did she go to the cops in San Francisco?" Rob asked.

Holly shrugged. "Maybe at first, she thought something had actually happened to him, and she simply had to know, before she could put any kind of plan to find him into motion."

"Makes sense," Coop said. "What we need here is a good old-fashioned DEA sting. Anybody have any suggestions?"

Logan tacked a clean sheet of paper to the bulletin board. "For starters, I think we should put a man in the suite next to Anna's. The balconies are separated by a gap and a railing, but close enough together to serve our purpose. I've already called Nick Von Sant at the hotel, and faxed him the photos. He said the suite next to Anna's is available. He also said he'd keep Anna under surveillance, and watch for Denado."

Rob frowned. "You guys still friends with Nikko Von Sant?"

Holly exchanged smiles with Logan. "Absolutely. I know when we visited you at Christmas time, I thought he was a miserable man, paraplegic or not, but all that changed when I found out who was trying to kill him, and why. We've become good friends."

Rob sighed. "Seems like a lifetime ago. I brought along my nifty camera."

Elima

"Then you're the best candidate for the stakeout at the hotel," Logan said, "because you've got your 'nifty,' complicated camera that nobody knows how to use but you. Maybe we'll get lucky and get a shot of Denado."

Buzzy spoke up. "Sounds like we'd better find Mario Rocettie before they do. And I don't give a hang if this Anna person hired St. James Investigations. Bet you anything she has Denado out looking for him, too."

Holly looked up at Buzzy's freckled face, and nodded. "That's right. And I don't think we have a moment to lose."

"This is going to take footwork, and lots of it," Logan said stoutly.

He was looking at Holly, and she knew what he was thinking. It would be best if she stayed out of it, and the look she gave him in return said, *"No way!"*

Logan sighed, put their names on the sheet of paper, and then listed their duties. "First thing tomorrow morning, I want you to check into the hotel, Rob, and start your surveillance. You'll have Nick and a few trusted hotel security officers to help you. Ty, Coop, I want the two of you to go to Anini Beach and poke around. Holly already checked with Max, and found out Mario's surfing friends said he was always on foot. That tells me he lived near the

98 *Georgette Livingston*

beach. Lots of vacation houses in the area, but some shanties, too. Knock on doors. Show Mario's photo to everyone you talk to. I'm going to spend the morning talking to his surfing friends. Got their addresses from Max, but I'll try Poipu Beach first. They said that's where they're going to surf from now on.''

Logan's golden-brown eyes settled on Holly. ''I don't have anything on the list for you and Buzzy to do, because I know you well enough, my love. You've already made your plans.''

Holly gave Logan a sly grin. ''Uh-huh. We're going to look for the vendor who supposedly sold Anna's friend the painting. He was selling his wares out of the back of a van on the beach. Doesn't matter *which* beach it was at the time, because vendors are always moving around. But if he's still on the island, we'll find him. And that won't take legwork, Logan. All we'll have to do is drive around.''

Logan nodded. ''Okay, and we'll keep in touch by radio, and meet back here sometime tomorrow afternoon. Now I think we should all try to get some sleep. We have sleeping bags and plenty of bedding, and enough food in the fridge to feed an army. I don't think you have to be told to make yourselves at home.''

Holly smiled, thinking about Tutu, and how pleased she was going to be she had the fore-

Elima 99

sight to air the bedding. Or what she was going to say in the morning, when she got up, and found bodies crashed all over the house. She could also picture the madhouse at breakfast, with Tutu insisting *nobody* was leaving the house without a decent meal, because *nobody*, not even Feds like Eliot Ness, could go out and do "cop stuff" on an empty stomach.

At the mention of food, the agents headed up the stairs. After they'd gone, Logan pulled Holly into his arms, and rained soft kisses over her face. "Are you going to bed now?"

"Hmm, I'm exhausted."

"Well, I won't be long. Tomorrow is going to be a big day. *Aloha au ia oe.*"

"I love you, too," she whispered, meaning it from the bottom of her heart.

The next morning, after a quick breakfast of toast and juice, much to Tutu's dismay, Holly and Buzzy were the first on the road. And they shared the same eagerness and excitement that always came when a big case was about to break. "We're going to get some answers today," she said, rolling down her window to the sweet morning air. "I can *feel* it."

"Yeah, me, too," Buzzy said, giving her a toothy grin. "Where to first?"

"I thought we'd start at Lydgate Park and

100   *Georgette Livingston*

work our way down to the southern tip of the island. When we see a vendor with a van, we'll stop. I want to stop by the office, too, and the gift shop, if we have the time. Jack and Cindy should be told what's going on. Poor Jack. Anna Rocettie has been driving him crazy.''

''And Cindy still has the artist's paintings on her wall?''

''Yes, and they really are quite beautiful. The man has a lot of talent. Wherever he's hiding, I'll bet he's painting.''

''Not if he's on the run,'' Buzzy said. ''You know, it's possible he's long gone. I mean, he could've faked the drowning and then split. Heck, he could be on the mainland by now.''

Holly thought about that as they headed south along the Kuhio Highway, and kept her fingers crossed that Mario was still on the island. Because if he wasn't, they would end up with an unsolved case, and no way to catch the culprits.

It was almost noon when they pulled into the parking area at Spouting Horn, where turquoise water exploded through black lava tube-like holes, gushing like a geyser. The spray was accompanied by sorrowful moans, said to be that of a legendary lizard who had been trapped in the tubes below. It was a great tour-

Elima 101

ist attraction, and it was also a good place for the vendors to sell their wares. So far, they had found only one van at Lydgate Park, and it had belonged to a couple of local kids. Buzzy had been in touch with the others by radio, and nobody had anything to report. Until now.

Holly cut the engine. "Do you see what I see?"

Buzzy took a deep breath. "Yeah, a blue van, and the guy is selling stuff out of the back."

With her heart up in her throat, Holly led the way across the sand, and gave the tall, unkempt man a warm smile. "Hi, there. How's business?"

The man shrugged. "Okay, I guess. I've got some abalone rings on sale today . . ."

Holly looked at the assortment of jewelry and shells spread out on a card table, and asked, "Do you ever sell paintings?"

The man, whose eyes had settled on Buzzy, noted his formidable size, and swallowed. "Yeah, sometimes, when I can get 'em."

Holly took in his frayed jeans and aloha shirt, and pulled a twenty-dollar bill out of her pocket. "How much for the shell necklace?"

"Three bucks."

She handed him the twenty. "You can keep the change if you'll give us some information.

102 *Georgette Livingston*

We're looking for a good friend. I received a postcard from him a few weeks ago, and he said he was on Kauai, and that a vendor was selling his paintings. But he didn't give me an address. Of course, he wasn't expecting me to fly over from the mainland. If you were the vendor who sold his paintings, I know you would remember them. Very lush and tropical. Swaying palms, that sort of thing. His name is Marty.''

The vendor smiled. ''Hey, yeah, I know Marty. Haven't seen him around, though. Guess the last time was a couple of weeks ago. I figured he left the island.''

Holly frowned. ''Boy, I hope not. I sold some of his paintings on the mainland, and I've got some money for him.''

''Me, too. That's why I thought it was funny when he didn't come back. You a vendor?''

''No, I own a gift shop. His paintings are so unique, they sell fast. Of course, you must know that.''

The vendor nodded. ''I know, but he never gave me that many to sell. The last one went to a couple from New York. Thought I had it sold before that, and for more money. See, Marty needed money. Anyway, it was some jerk who asked a dozen questions, but wouldn't open his

Elima 103

wallet. Wouldn't even crack the lousy thing. I came down in price, too.''

''Why was he asking questions?''

''Don't know. Jerk. He was wearing a diamond ring the size of a rock. I knew he had money, and I knew he was interested in the painting.''

''Is this the man?'' Holly said, handing the vendor the photo of Frank Denado.

He looked at it and nodded, and then scowled. ''You wanna level with me?''

Holly took a deep breath, and handed him a hundred-dollar bill. ''I can't go into details, except to say Marty is in trouble, and it's imperative we find him.''

The man's eyes flickered up and down Holly's Hawaiian print sundress and the golden tan of her skin, and muttered, ''You ain't from the mainland.''

''No, I'm not. Can you remember if you saw Marty after that man was here?''

''Yeah, one more time. The next day, I think. He stopped by to see if I had sold his painting, 'cause he needed the money. I took his stuff on consignment, see. We'd divvy up the money after a painting was sold.''

''And did you tell him about the man who was asking questions?''

The vendor nodded.

104   *Georgette Livingston*

"What did Marty say?"

"Nothing, but he didn't look too happy about it."

"Do you remember what kind of questions the man asked?"

"Stuff like, if I knew where the artist lived. Said he was interested in buying all his work. Ticked me off, 'cause then I wouldn't get a cut. So what happens? I couldn't get him to buy the painting I had, and figured him for a flake."

"Have you seen the man in the photo since?"

"Nope."

"Were you here at Spouting Horn at the time?"

"Yeah. I'm always here. This is the best spot. Lots of tourists."

"Do you remember if Marty had a vehicle?"

"Yeah. A beat-up motor scooter on its last legs. He asked me if I knew a good mechanic who could fix it up for a fair price. Told him about Sammy Kalama in Hanapepe."

"Sammy has a garage?"

"Yeah. It ain't much, but he does a good business. He's fixed my van a couple of times."

Elima 105

"Can you remember the color of the motor scooter?"

"Black and white."

"Did you tell the man about the motor scooter?"

"Nope. Never did. Might have, if he'd asked."

Holly handed the man another hundred-dollar bill, and a business card. "If you happen to see Marty again, I'd appreciate a call. Tell him I'm a friend, and I'm trying to help him. If you see that man again, or this woman—" She handed him Anna's photo. "—I'd appreciate it if you didn't say anything about this conversation."

The vendor took the money and card, and looked at the photo. "I haven't seen her."

"Okay, but we can't leave anything to chance. Thanks for all your help. *Aloha*."

Holly and Buzzy had reached the Blazer when the vendor caught up with them. "You forgot this," he said, handing her the shell necklace.

Holly smiled. "The necklace is lovely, but you keep it. And you should be charging twenty dollars for it instead of three."

Holly pulled out on the road, and tried to contain her excitement. "We're going to find

106   *Georgette Livingston*

him, Buzzy. It might not be today, or tomorrow, but we're going to find him!''

''I'd give anything for a bag of gumdrops right about now,'' Buzzy said forlornly.

''Me, too. How much do you want to bet Mario planned his demise the minute he heard about the man? He had to know it was Denado, and probably figured his wife was on the island, too.''

''So why didn't he take off?'' Buzzy asked. ''Flights leave for Oahu all day long, and it's a big world out there.''

''Maybe he didn't have the money. The vendor said he sold the painting to a couple from New York after he talked to Mario that last time, and he hasn't seen Mario since, to give him the money. Maybe Mario didn't want to chance coming back, no matter how desperate for money he was.''

''So now what?''

''We're going to talk to the mechanic in Hanapepe. If he fixed the motor scooter, he might have an address. You don't need a driver's license to zip around on a motor scooter in the islands, so the Department of Motor Vehicles wouldn't have that information.''

''Want to call Logan?''

''Let's wait until after we talk to the mechanic.''

Elima 107

Buzzy nodded, and stared out the window, and she knew what he was thinking. So close, and yet they still had a long way to go.

The garage was near the Green Garden Restaurant, and Buzzy closed his eyes as they drove by. "You'll have dinner with us tonight," Holly said with a grin, "to make up for our day of starvation. I'll call Tutu after I call Logan, and tell her to make it extra special."

"You're on," Buzzy muttered. "I know I'm on a diet, but even that has its limitations."

They found Sammy in the back of the cluttered garage, eating a sandwich. He was a nice-looking island man, with dark hair and eyes, or would have been if it wasn't for all the grease on his skin and clothing. He stood up, and grinned. "You need some work done on the Blazer?"

Holly shook her head. "We just want to ask you a few questions, Mr. Kalama. We were talking to a vendor on the beach, and he gave us your name, and told us where to find you."

"Blue van?"

"Yes."

"That's Pete. Nice *haole*."

"We're looking for a man who goes by the name of Marty. He's an artist, and—"

108 *Georgette Livingston*

The grin widened. "Yeah, I know Marty. Wanted me to fix his motor scooter, but didn't have the money. I said he could owe me, but he wouldn't do it. Said he always pays his bills up front."

Holly exchanged glances with Buzzy. "Did he say where he's staying?"

"Nope, but he was walkin'. Said the scooter conked out."

"And you haven't seen him since?"

"Nope."

"Well, thanks," Holly said dejectedly.

When they were in the Blazer, Holly muttered, "Don't say it, I'll say it for you. Now what?"

"I'd say if he was on foot, then he has to be staying around here somewhere, Holly. You have your gut feelings, and I have mine. I say we start looking for a black-and-white scooter."

Holly sighed. "Right. Like he's going to leave it out in the open."

"He might," Buzzy said thoughtfully. "If he knows Denado doesn't know about it." He looked out at the historic old town of Hanapepe nestled along the Hanapepe River, and said, "You know what we've got here? Dozens of wooden buildings, overhanging the river, with lots of rooms for rent. Little dirt roads, houses

Elima 109

tucked into the side of the hills, farmland beyond, and tradition. A way of life that goes back hundreds of years. We go poking around here and start knocking on doors, we're not gonna get a friendly welcome.''

''Well, we'll have to chance it,'' Holly said, starting the Blazer.

At that moment, Sammy walked up to the open driver's window and cleared his throat. ''Ah, I, uh, I remember somethin'. Marty said when he got the money to fix the scooter, he'd be back. I asked him how he was gonna get it here if it wasn't running, and he said it wouldn't be no problem. He'd just give it a shove down the hill, and it would end up in my backyard.'' He looked up the hill behind the garage. ''I know he was trying to be funny, but . . .''

Holly got out of the Blazer, and looked up the hill behind the garage. ''What's up there?''

''Nothin' much. A few old houses. Most of them empty. The road dead-ends.''

''Which road?''

''About a quarter of a mile down. Just before you get to the end of this road. Ain't much. Full of ruts.''

Holly thanked the man, and climbed in the Blazer. But she didn't comment until they'd pulled away. ''This is it, Buzzy. I can feel it

110   *Georgette Livingston*

in every fiber of my being. He's staying in one of those empty houses. It would be a perfect place to hide.''

Buzzy opened his mouth, and closed it, and didn't respond until they'd turned off the main road. And then, ''He might run, Holly. We go to the front door, and he might go right out the back.''

Holly reasoned, ''But there are two of us and only one of him. I'll wait until you're around back before I knock on the door.''

''And if he doesn't open the door?''

''We'll worry about that when we get there.''

''I think I'd rather worry about it now,'' Buzzy said as the Blazer bounced over the ruts in the road. '' 'Cause this ain't gonna work unless we've got some sort of a foolproof plan.''

''I'll tell him I'm a cop, and he's under arrest.''

Buzzy groaned. ''Terrific. You're the one who will end up in the slammer for impersonating a police officer. Want a file in your cake when I visit you in jail?''

Holly giggled, and slowed the vehicle for the next supersized rut. And all the while, her heart was pounding in her ears. They were so close, and this time, they only had a mile or so to go.

Chapter Seven

At the top of the hill, though a small lane snaked off to the right, the road itself came to an abrupt end, but left enough room for Holly to turn the Blazer around. That done, she backed up under a tangle of vines and eucalyptus trees, and cut the engine. "I think we'd better go the rest of the way on foot, Buzzy. We don't want to frighten Mario off before we can get to the house."

Buzzy nodded. "Are you packing?"

"I always carry my .38, Buzzy. You know that."

"Yeah, well, keep it handy. For all we know, he's got an arsenal ready and waiting. I would, if I thought somebody wanted to kill

112 *Georgette Livingston*

me. And we can't forget he might be one of the bad guys."

"He isn't, and I'd bet my life on it," Holly said, climbing out of the Blazer. She took a deep breath. The warm afternoon air was fresh, washed clean by the slight breeze coming in off the river. She reached behind the front seat and pulled out a pair of sneakers, and then with the door open, sat down on the driver's seat to remove her sandals. She was tying the sneakers when Buzzy walked around the Blazer to join her, and she could see the merriment dancing in his eyes. "I know," she muttered. "Sneakers and a sundress. Not a fashion statement. But that lane isn't much more than a weed-covered trail, and who knows what it's like further on." She adjusted her sunglasses on the bridge of her nose, made sure the Blazer was locked, and took Buzzy's arm. "Did I ever tell you about the first time I met Logan?"

Buzzy grinned. "No. Were you wearing sneakers and a sundress?"

"I was wearing jeans and a blouse, actually. I'd been following him all over the island for days, thinking he was the two-timing husband I'd been hired to follow."

Buzzy chuckled. "Logan told me about that, and how you were in the middle of a DEA sting operation, and didn't know it."

Elima 113

"Uh-huh, but the point is, I had to follow him into a fancy restaurant wearing jeans. Then later, he confronted me in the parking lot, and basically told me that if I was going to follow somebody around, I had better keep my red hair covered. From that day on, I've always carried an assortment of clothing and stuff with me, no matter where I go. Even have a couple of wigs, in the event I want to cover up my red tresses.''

They had reached a slight rise, and the view was spectacular. Below them, they could see the main road, the settlement, and the dark, green river. Beyond, taro patches spread out for miles, and then the blue Pacific, looking like a smooth lake in the distance.

To their right, a driveway wound up through a stand of koa trees, and ended at a shack with the windows boarded up. Buzzy examined the dirt driveway, and shook his head. "No footprints or tire tracks. This ain't the place."

They moved on, concentrating now on every detail around them.

When Buzzy stopped to wipe the perspiration from his brow, he said, "Ahead of us at two o'clock, Holly. No, look down."

Holly saw the little house, perched precariously on the side of the hill, and far below it, Sammy's garage. Everything seemed to accel-

114　　*Georgette Livingston*

erate. Her breath, her pulse, her pounding heart, because she could also see the black-and-white motor scooter, tucked in under a silver oak tree. No driveway, but a winding path led down to the house.

And then she saw Mario, sitting on the porch. Long hair and a beard, just like Cindy had described. He was wearing cutoff jeans and an aloha shirt, and she could see the defeated, lonely slump to his shoulders.

Holly pulled Buzzy back in the shadow of a tree, and whispered, "It's Mario. He's sitting on the front porch! Okay, what do we do now? There is no way you can get around behind the house. You'd end up in Sammy's backyard."

"Good thinking on his part," Buzzy said. "No way anybody is gonna sneak in from the rear."

Holly took a deep breath. "I have to get to him while he's still outside, Buzzy. And I have to make it look good." She pulled the pins out of her hair and let it tumble around her shoulders. Buzzy watched in amazement as she wiped the makeup off her face with a tissue, replaced it with smudges of dirt, and took off her sneakers. "I'd rip my dress if it wasn't one of my favorites," she said, grinning up at him. "So what do you think?"

"I think you're crazy," Buzzy grumbled.

Elima 115

"He could shoot you before you get halfway down the trail."

"He could, but I don't think he will. I'm going on the assumption Mario Rocettie is a good guy, Buzzy. I want you to stay out of sight until I talk to him. When I have everything under control, I'll wave."

"You're gonna break a toe, running around barefoot . . ."

"My feet are tough. That comes from years of going without shoes. Even when I was a kid, I didn't wear shoes unless I had to."

"Holly—"

"It's the only way," Holly broke in. "One look at you, and Mario would freak out on general principles."

Buzzy ran a hand through his spiky blond hair. "Logan is gonna kill me when he finds out about this."

"Uh-huh, but he doesn't have to find out, unless you tell him. When you hear me scream, don't panic. It's all part of the plan."

"You've managed to come up with a plan already?" Buzzy asked incredulously.

"Sort of." She gave Buzzy a hug, and made her way up the road. When she reached the path and realized the porch was obscured by trees, which meant Mario couldn't see her, either, Holly stopped long enough to catch her

116   *Georgette Livingston*

breath and formulate her next move. She looked back at Buzzy. He was on red alert, and resembled a cat about to spring. She gave him a nonchalant wave, but she knew how he felt. She had no idea if this was going to work, and if it didn't . . . Holly shook her head, refused to accept failure, and looked down the trail. At about the halfway point, it jogged to the right, and was bathed in sunlight. And that was where Mario would be able to see her. And that was where she would have to make her grand entrance.

Holly proceeded down, holding her breath now, until she felt her lungs might explode. One step, then two. When she stepped on a rock, she nearly cried out, and then decided to use that to her advantage, because she only had a few more feet left to go. She scooted along down on her haunches until she reached the sunlight. Then she began moaning. "Ahh, ohh, somebody help me!" Screams followed, and deep wails, while she sat crumpled on the pathway, holding her ankle.

When she stopped to take a breath, she could hear Mario muttering, but she could also hear his approaching footsteps. Cries of agony again as she squeezed her eyes shut, trying to produce tears.

Elima 117

"What the heck is going on?" Mario demanded when he reached her.

Holly looked up at him, trying to decide if his dark eyes held anger or concern, and knew the next few moments would be all that mattered, because she wasn't going to get a second chance. "I was looking at some property down the road, and fell. Ohh, it's my ankle! Ouch! I fell down into some sort of a gully, and had to crawl out. Ahh . . . ohh . . . ! I was trying to get back to my car, when I saw your house. Ohh . . ." Holly moaned and closed her eyes. She felt one lonely tear slip down her cheek, and hoped it was mixing with the dirt on her face.

Mario made no move to help her up, but asked, "Where's your car?"

"Ohh . . . ahh . . . it's way down there," Holly said, flailing an arm in the general direction.

Mario cursed under his breath, and in the next breath, scooped her up in his arms and carried her down the trail to the house. He was very strong, and he was very angry, but Holly knew in her heart he wasn't going to harm her.

When they reached the rickety porch, he placed her in a worn cane chair, and muttered,

118 *Georgette Livingston*

"Don't move. I'm getting you a glass of water."

Holly looked up the hill, caught movement through the undergrowth, and knew it was Buzzy. By the time Mario had returned with the water, she was wearing a woebegone expression, and had managed to squeeze out another tear. She took the glass of water, clung to it, and moaned.

"Put your foot up," Mario mumbled, shoving a pineapple crate in front of her.

Holly put her foot up, took a sip of water, and uttered a ragged gasp. Then another, before she said, "I-I'm so sorry for bothering you, but I felt faint, and then . . ."

Mario shook his head. "Accidents happen." He examined her ankle. "Doesn't seem to be broken, and there isn't much swelling."

Holly finished the water and handed him the glass. "It was really stupid of me to try this without shoes."

Mario studied her intently for a few moments before he said, "You're not a tourist."

It wasn't a question, it was a statement. "Oh, no," Holly said. "I live on Kauai. I've lived here nearly all my life. That's why this was so stupid. I know what this area is like, and so I should have worn shoes." Another moan.

Elima 119

"What property were you looking at?" Mario asked.

Holly waved a hand. "Down there. Five acres, but I couldn't find a sign. Now I'm wondering if I'm on the right road."

"If I get you to your car, do you think you can drive?"

"Yes, but I couldn't expect you to carry me *that* far . . ."

Mario ran a hand through his long, dark hair. "Well, maybe I can find something for you to use as a crutch, and then with me supporting you on one side . . ."

Holly took a deep breath. She couldn't let this go on one more minute. She reached in her tote, pulled out a business card, and handed it to him. "My name is Holly St. James. I'm a private investigator. Your wife hired me to find you, Mario, but I think she's trying to kill you, and I'm on your side." It all came out in one big swoosh, and then she took a deep breath again, and held it.

At first Mario looked like a frightened deer caught in the headlights of a speeding vehicle. And just as quickly, anger replaced the fear. She thought for a moment he might run, so she quickly said, "I meant what I said, Mario. Your wife is on the island with a very bad man, and I think if they find you, they'll kill you.

120 *Georgette Livingston*

I'm married to Logan West, a DEA agent. As we speak, your wife is under surveillance, and agents are all over the island, looking for you, because you need protection.''

Mario sat down on the steps and held his head in his hands. ''Should've tried swimming to Oahu,'' he muttered. ''I knew my days were numbered.''

Holly got up and sat down beside him. ''But they aren't numbered, Mario. You'll be safe with us, and with a little bit of luck, we can catch your wife and Frank Denado, and put them behind bars where they belong.''

Mario shook his head. ''So, you know who you're dealing with.''

''Frank Denado? Yes.'' Holly reached into her tote and pulled out the photos. ''We received these by fax from San Francisco, along with a report. Denado is a wanted man. Only thing is, nobody seems to know how to catch him.''

Mario glanced at the photos and tossed them aside. ''Analisa Newfall, huh? So that's her real name. Man, what a trip. I thought she loved me . . .''

''She's a very good actress, Mario. She had us fooled at the beginning, too. And although we know who we're dealing with, there are still a good many unanswered questions. But

Elima 121

first, I'd better tell you, I didn't come alone. A friend is with me. His name is Buzzy Caghorn. He's going to be a cop someday, and I'd trust him with my life.''

Mario looked around. ''So where is he?''

''Up on the road, waiting for my signal. We thought it would be best if I approached you alone. He's a very large man. Intimidating, though he's a pussycat inside . . .''

Mario looked down at her ankle, and for the first time, a light twinkled in his eyes. ''And the ankle bit?''

''My ankle is fine, Mario.''

''How did you find me?''

''We'll get to all that in a few minutes, but first, let's get Buzzy down here, and go inside. You might feel safe enough here, but I don't want to leave anything to chance.''

Holly stood up and waved at Buzzy, who wasted no time getting down the path, sliding and kicking up a mountain of dust. Nor did they waste any time getting into the house.

Mario motioned with a hand. ''Sit where you can. I'm a little short on furniture.''

Although the living room was nearly empty but for a few crates and boxes, it was clean, and sunlight spilled through the windows. The windows were open to the island breeze, too, and flowers stuffed in jelly glasses filled every

122 *Georgette Livingston*

corner. The sight of them brought an unexpected lump to Holly's throat. The man was in hiding, and yet he'd tried to make the shabby house a home.

Holly and Buzzy sat down on crates, but Mario remained standing. He still looked uncomfortable, and Holly tried to put him at ease. "Sit down, Mario. I think I can truthfully say for the first time in three months, you can relax. We're here, you're safe, and you don't have to keep looking over your shoulder."

"Force of habit," Mario muttered. "Haven't got much to drink. Some juice, or water . . ."

"We're fine," Holly told him. "I think the first thing we should do is get you out of here. I know, I just said you were safe, but why take chances?"

"This is about the safest place for me on the island," Mario said dismally.

"Second safest place," Holly said. "My house will be safer. My husband has state-of-the-art surveillance equipment, a high-tech security system, and law enforcement friends who know what they're doing. Which reminds me." She pulled the portable radio from her tote, and keyed the mike. "Hollyberry one to Loganberry two."

A few moments later, Logan's voice crack-

Elima 123

led over the radio. "Loganberry two, go ahead, Hollyberry one."

"The chickens have come home to roost."

"Ten-four, Hollyberry one. Over and out."

Holly put the radio in her tote, and said, "That was my husband. I just wanted him to know we'd found you, and all the agents can call it a day."

Mario shook his head. "Cop stuff. Who would've believed it?"

Buzzy grinned. "That's the way I felt at the beginning. It's overwhelming at first, but you'll get used to it."

"How long do you think it'll take to get your things together?" Holly asked. "I know you're traveling light, but . . ."

"Everything would fit in a box."

"Food? If you've stocked your shelves . . ."

Mario laughed without humor. "A couple of cans of soup, a stale loaf of bread, and a bag of oranges. Life has been meager at best."

"What about your scooter? I know it isn't running, but—"

This time, Mario's laugh was genuine. "I think I can leave it behind without remorse. How did you find out about the scooter?"

"Pete, the vendor at Spouting Horn. He told us about Sammy Kalama, and Sammy said *you* said if you ever got the money together to fix

124 *Georgette Livingston*

the scooter, all you'd have to do was roll it down the hill, and it would end up in his backyard. At that point, we decided you had to be living up here somewhere, and probably in one of the empty houses.''

''Hmm, guess that's why you're a P.I. Well, I'd like you to know, I'm not a squatter. The owner of this wonderful abode lives on Niihau, and only gets over once a year. He happened to be here the day I was looking for a place to stay, and took pity on a beach bum without a penny in his pocket. He said I could stay here until he made arrangements to sell the property, and the way he talked, that might be years.'' His face darkened. ''If you could figure it out, Anna—excuse me, Analisa—and her corrupt partner could figure it out, too.''

''I don't think so, Mario. Pete, the vendor, told us about the man who was interested in your painting, and asking all the questions. I showed the vendor the photos, and he said he hadn't seen Anna at all, and hasn't seen the man since the last time he talked to you. He said he told you about the man, so I knew *you* knew they were on the island. Is that why you planned your own death?''

Mario shook his head. ''You're smart, Miss St. James. Very smart. Yes, that's why I did it. I panicked. I knew if they found me, they'd

Elima 125

kill me. I was living in a little cottage on Anini Beach at the time, and had made friends with three local kids. We didn't have much in common except surfing. That particular day, the surf was high. Too high.''

"But you went out anyway," Holly said. "And that's when you faked the accident, and disappeared."

"That's right. I'm a good swimmer, but I still had one heck of a time swimming in, but I managed to hit the beach a little further south, and make my way back to the cottage. The kids knew me as Marty Ricco, but I'd rented the cottage as Ricco Martin, and the kids didn't know where I was staying. The rent was paid up until the end of the month, so I just took off. The scooter was in lousy shape, and I held my breath the whole way. What I wanted to do was just drive right off the island, but I couldn't. Couldn't take a plane, either, because I was nearly broke. I spent the first night in a cave on the beach, and found this place the next day. Unfortunately, I've been in a no-win situation. Out in the open, I could get my head blown off, and being holed up here could mean eventual starvation. Riffling through garbage cans actually came to mind.''

His jaw had tightened, and the pain in his eyes was acute. Holly felt her heart twist.

126 *Georgette Livingston*

"Well, I don't think you have to worry about the vendor saying anything, if in fact your wife or Denado show up. I gave him a healthy amount of money to keep him quiet. But really, it doesn't matter now. If you'll get your things together . . ."

Mario stood up, and started to pace. "I think I'd better tell you why I left San Francisco in such a hurry, Miss St. James. It might make a difference. You might want to change your plans."

"Not unless you're going to tell us you're an ax murderer."

He gave her a wan smile. "No, nothing like that, but what I did . . ." He heaved a sigh.

"Why don't I tell you what we know, Mario, and then you take it from there?" When he nodded, Holly hurried on, reciting what Anna had told her, what they'd received on the fax, and what they'd put together from their own observations.

Mario kept nodding his head, or shaking his head, and then, "Most of it is true. I married Anna last March. I was already the curator of the art gallery, and pretty happy with my work. The owner was about to retire, and had talked to me about buying the gallery. But I was dragging my feet. Even though it was a good deal,

Elima 127

I didn't have much money. I was afraid of getting in over my head."

"Where were you living at the time?" Holly asked.

"In a one-room studio on Telegraph Hill. Then in February, Anna walked in, and changed my life. She was beautiful. Classy, and very sophisticated. She said she was looking for a particular painting. We didn't have it at the gallery, but she hung around. By the end of the day, I'd invited her out to dinner, and things just escalated from there. I can't say it was love at first sight on my part, but it was close. I'd had a few disappointing relationships, and Anna was like a breath of fresh air."

"Fresh air filled with poison gas," Buzzy muttered. "So you married her."

"Three weeks later. Looking back, I can see she was setting me up, even then. But they say love is blind. We didn't go on a honeymoon because I couldn't get away from the gallery. We spent our wedding night in her apartment on Russian Hill. She said she was subletting it from a friend."

Holly sighed. "Frank Denado."

"That's right, only I didn't know it at the time. Anyway, it wasn't long before she asked me if I'd ever thought about buying the art gallery. She had observed the owner was ancient,

128 *Georgette Livingston*

and more than ready to retire. I told her about the owner's offer, and she told me to go for it. She said she had lots of money, so I could quit dragging my feet. I refused to let her help, and bought the gallery in June. Nearly wiped me out, but she painted a pretty picture. She kept saying, 'What's mine is yours.' We opened a joint checking account, and although I never saw any big money, she always kept the balance at a certain amount. Even if the gallery had a bad month. I think she was just trying to pacify me. The fact that she never spent any money on me personally didn't occur to me until later. It was always for the art gallery. Not that I expected it.''

''Did you ever wonder where she was getting the money she was putting into the bank account?'' Buzzy asked.

''Sure I did, but I figured it was her business. I've never much believed in that 'what's mine is yours' stuff. I wanted to make a go of the gallery on my own, and basically, she *was* my pacifier. At least I knew I wouldn't starve.''

''Did you see Denado during that time?'' Holly asked.

''No, and she never mentioned him. And then . . . In early November, Anna came into the gallery one afternoon, and said she'd heard

Elima 129

from a friend in Europe who could cut me a deal on some lithographs by a well-known artist. The markup would be substantial, so I thought it was a good idea. Even better, the lithographs were already mounted and framed. She suggested I order at least twenty, but I didn't have the money, so I ordered ten. She even knew when they would arrive, and planned to be in the gallery that day. Well, that's where things got screwed up. They arrived three days earlier than expected. I would have called Anna, because I knew she wanted to be there for the unveiling, but that was the day she was in San Jose, having lunch with a 'friend.' I knew I should wait, but I felt like a kid on Christmas morning, so I went ahead and opened up the crate. The lithographs were lovely, and I was very pleased. I planned to put several out front on display, and was trying to figure out where to store the rest, when I realized I had eleven instead of ten. I checked the packing slip, but it said ten, and I'd paid for ten. It wasn't a big deal, because I knew I could always settle the matter later, but there was something about that last lithograph in the crate that drew my attention.''

Holly was shaking her head. ''Uh-oh.''

''Uh-oh, is right. It was heavier, for one thing, and when I put it up to the light, there

130 *Georgette Livingston*

was a denseness about it that I couldn't detect in the others. It occurred to me then that there had to be something underneath the lithograph. I closed the gallery and removed the frame. Thinking about it now, I'm surprised I didn't keel over in a dead faint. I knew what I was looking at, but my mind wouldn't accept it. I might be a ho-hum artist, but I know paintings. I'd heard of the theft two years before. Happened in Paris. Some very nervy and creative thief had lifted a priceless painting right out of a gallery. It was 'Summer' by the seventeenth-century French master Jacques Jenot.''

Holly felt her hands trembling. ''We received that information on the fax, and that Denado was thought to be the mastermind.''

Mario stopped pacing and sat down. ''I had no proof it was *the* painting, of course; it could have been a copy, and at that point in time, I still didn't suspect Anna. My first thought was to call Bert, the ex-owner, but I knew he was vacationing in New York. Next thought was to call the cops. But then I got to thinking. *I* was the one who had ordered the lithographs. Did that make me an accomplice? To tell you the truth, I had a headache that wouldn't end, and I didn't know what to do.

''I finally decided to wait for Anna. She said she would stop by the gallery on her way home

Elima 131

from San Jose, so I made a pot of coffee, kept the gallery closed, and spent the worst couple of hours of my life, waiting. When Anna banged on the back door around four, I was a wreck. At first she wanted to know why everything was locked up, and then she saw the painting, and I'll never forget the look on her face. Mouth open, eyes glazed, cheeks that were flushed one minute and turned pale the next. I told her what had happened while she recovered, but when I asked her if she thought I should call the cops, she went into a snit, and wanted to know if I'd lost my mind. She reminded me that *I* had ordered the lithographs, and knowing how the authorities worked, I'd probably be behind bars before the evening news. All she did was substantiate my original fears, and I was frantic. Anna said she knew somebody in Europe, somebody *big,* who could give us advice, and that she would go home and call him. I wanted to know why she couldn't make the call from the gallery, and she said the person wasn't exactly a favorite in the world of law enforcement, and that she wanted to make the call in private.

"I wasn't thinking with a clear head, of course, or maybe I would've seen the truth in her eyes. Maybe I would've been able to put it together. In any event, she said she wanted

132 *Georgette Livingston*

me to stay at the gallery with the painting, and keep the doors locked. She didn't even want me to answer the phone. She said that after she talked to her friend, she would call me. She'd ring twice, hang up, and call again. That would be my signal it was her. I agreed, of course, but about a half hour after she left, I knew it wasn't going to work. I actually thought I was going to have a heart attack. All I could think about was spending the rest of my life in jail. The painting, though small in size, was worth a fortune, and every agency in the world was looking for it.

"I put the painting, with the lithograph on top, back in the frame, and drove home. That was an experience, too. I kept looking over my shoulder, and wondering what would happen if I was involved in an accident. When I finally walked into the apartment—even managing the steps was an experience because my legs felt like solid cement—I was about to call for Anna, but then I heard her voice. She was talking on the phone in the kitchen, had her voice raised, and obviously hadn't heard me come in. And her words were chilling. 'He'll be at the gallery until I call him, Frank, and he hasn't a clue. All you have to do is stop by here and get the key to the back door, let yourself into the gallery, and blow him away. Take a couple

Elima 133

of the lithographs to make it look like a robbery, and we're home free. No way. I'm not going to do it. Oh, right, the big Frank Denado doesn't want to get his hands dirty. Give me a break! I know you miss our little love nest on Russian Hill, but think of all the money we'll have when this is over!'

"I hurried out, drove down the hill, and knew I had to run. At that moment, I had no plan, and felt only a deep sense of regret, and anger. Anna had set me up. She married me to get access to the gallery, and my life, so that when the time came to order the lithographs, I would do her bidding. She had her patsy. It was all clear in an instant. She said she wanted to be at the gallery when the lithographs arrived, and I knew why. When the extra print turned up, she had planned to take it home. She probably planned to pay for it. And then? I can only guess. More than likely, she would've taken off with the painting, and Frank Denado.''

"And I can guess what happened after that,'' Holly said. "You got on the first plane for Hawaii.''

"That's right, but not until I stopped by the gallery. I cleaned out the small safe I had in the back room. It contained two days' worth of receipts. A total of two thousand and some

134 *Georgette Livingston*

pocket change. I left my car in the parking lot, walked three blocks, and caught a cab. All I had was the money, the shirt on my back, and the painting, wrapped up in butcher paper. When I got to the airport, I had no idea where I was going. But the next flight out was winging its way to Honolulu in a couple of minutes, and they had several seats left.''

Mario's story was incredible, but there was one big question he hadn't addressed. ''Do you have any idea how they ended up on Kauai?'' Holly asked finally. ''Anna said a friend bought a painting from a vendor on the beach, took it back to San Francisco, and she recognized it as your work.''

''I'm afraid it wasn't that simple. I think it was a long shot for them, but one that paid off. When we were married, and couldn't take a honeymoon, I told her that someday we'd go to the island of Oahu, and spend a month in the sun. I told her it had been my dream for years, and that nothing pleased me more than the thought of spending lazy days painting, and romancing her in the moonlight. It was my idea of bliss. I remembered telling her that, when I stepped off the plane in Honolulu. I got on the next plane for Kauai, and we can only speculate on the rest. I think when she remembered how much I wanted to visit Hawaii, they were

Elima 135

on the next plane. And maybe they decided to start on the outer islands, and work their way back to Oahu. I think she knew that no matter where I was, I'd be painting. Guess I'd better tell you. The vendor on the beach isn't the only person who was selling my paintings. I gave some to an art gallery.''

''I know. That's how I found out about you. A good friend of mine owns the gallery, Mario, and she told me about your accident. Right after that, your wife showed up and hired St. James Investigations to find you. And money was no object. I told her I thought Marty Ricco and Mario Rocettie were one and the same, and I told her about the surfing accident. But she refused to believe you were dead, and even went so far as to say you might have gotten bonked on the head and were walking around the island with amnesia.

''But, because I'm a P.I., and well trained when it comes to lies and deceit, I didn't buy her story. We did some checking, and you know the rest.''

''Except how you plan to catch them,'' Mario said dejectedly.

''To tell you the truth, I don't know. Our first priority was to find you. Now that we have, we can focus on some sort of a sting operation. How that's handled will be up to my

136 *Georgette Livingston*

husband and his DEA buddies. But I can tell you this much. They are very good.''

Buzzy cleared his throat. "I have a dumb question. What happened to the painting?''

Mario cast his eyes downward, and he flushed. "I have it. After all this time, I still don't know what to do with it.''

Holly smiled. "Well, for starters, you can stop worrying about retribution. When the authorities hear your story, they'll believe, as I do, that you were an innocent victim.

"Now, I think we should be on our way.'' She looked at Mario slyly. "It's daylight, but I don't want to wait until dark. We shouldn't take any chances driving through Lihue. Are you up for a disguise?''

He stroked his beard. "This isn't enough?''

"No, it isn't. Anna knows you have long hair and a beard. My friend at the gallery spilled the beans. Innocent mistake. But I have a short blond wig in my car that might work. It's stretchy. One size fits all, and we can cover up your beard with a scarf.''

Mario shook his head, like he couldn't believe this was happening, and went into the bedroom to pack.

Chapter Eight

Because they had gotten bogged down in traffic, and stuck behind an accident on the Kuhio Highway for nearly twenty minutes, it had been a hectic drive home at best. The only highlight had been Mario's surprised expression when Holly turned off the highway into the maze of cane fields. Finally, he'd gotten up the courage to ask, "Where are we going?" Buzzy had been the first to answer, and by the time they reached the house, Mario had received a colorful accounting of Buzzy's first visit to the estate. An experience, he claimed, that had left him speechless for days. Mario seemed amused until the house came into view.

138 *Georgette Livingston*

At that point, all he could do was shake his head and utter, "Wow, will you look at that!"

Sitting in the kitchen now, while Tutu bustled around fixing dinner, Holly smiled, thinking about his reaction. And she remembered how she'd felt the first time she'd seen the magnificent sprawling structure, which was a mélange of Mediterranean and Polynesian architectural styles. She also thought about all those incredible days that followed. . . .

Tutu was speaking to her, and Holly blinked. "I'm sorry, Tutu?"

Tutu waved a spoon in Holly's direction. "I said, you are tired. It has been a long day."

"Yes, it has. I hope you were able to get some rest."

Tutu grinned. "Men gone, easy day. Boring. Now things pick up, yeah. That *haolekane* is innocent. Warm eyes. Nice smile. Handsome, if he'd shave off that beard."

She was talking about Mario who, at the moment, was repeating his amazing story to the agents in Logan's office. Buzzy was sitting in on the meeting, too, but all Holly had wanted to do after they'd gotten home was shower and change her clothes. It seemed as though she'd been gone days, instead of only a few hours, and she needed this time to unwind. "Yes, he

Elima 139

is innocent, Tutu, and we were lucky to find him so quickly.''

Tutu nodded. ''Now they make plans to catch the bad guys?''

''Yes, but it isn't going to be easy. They're going to have to set up some sort of a sting operation to flush them out.''

''They will think better after a good meal,'' Tutu announced. ''Poi, *lomi lomi, lau lau,* chicken long rice, and *haupia,* yeah.''

Holly mentally translated. Poi was a pasty pudding from pulverized taro root. Lomi lomi was shredded salmon mixed with tomatoes and green onions. Lau lau was a steamed dish with spicy meat wrapped in taro leaves, and chicken long rice was actually a long transparent noodle. For dessert, they were having a rich coconut pudding called *haupia*. Kona coffee would complement the meal. Fortunately, she had heeded Buzzy's advice, and had eaten a sandwich upon their arrival, or her stomach would be grumbling unmercifully.

''But first, you will begin with *pupus*,'' Tutu said, pulling two trays of appetizers out of the refrigerator. ''Crackers, cheese, fish, and don't ask about the rest. You will eat on the terrace by the light of the tiki torches, and it will be a festive occasion, yeah.''

A few minutes later, Mario walked into the

140   *Georgette Livingston*

kitchen to tell Holly the meeting was over, and that Logan was preparing some drinks.

"So, how did the meeting go?" Holly asked.

Mario shrugged. "Okay, I guess. I got lost a couple of times with all the cop jargon, but I have no doubt they know what they're doing. They've set up a plan, but you'd better ask your husband about it. He made a few calls, but you'd better ask him about that, too. The whole thing is way over my head. This is some house, Miss St. James . . . or is it Mrs. West?"

"It's Holly. I think we've gotten beyond formality. My brother and I own St. James Investigations, and it's easier to use my maiden name when I'm working on a case. The rest of the time, I'm Holly West."

Tutu was in full swing now, scooting here and rushing there. Mario shook his head. "That lady is something else, too. Do you think she'd be upset if I offered to help?"

"I think she'd be delighted. Not because she wants help, or needs it, but because she likes you. She said you'd be very handsome if you shaved off your beard. She should have seen you earlier, wearing that blond wig."

Mario chuckled, walked over to Tutu, and whispered something in her ear. Tutu beamed.

Holly smiled, and went in search of Logan.

Elima 141

She found him in the living room with Ty, Coop, and Buzzy, where he was serving the drinks at the portable bar.

"Well?" Holly said, climbing up on a bar stool. "Mario said you made a few calls, and have everything planned out."

Logan nodded. "Hopefully, it works. Would you like a drink, my love?"

"Just soda, I think. I haven't had much to eat today."

"I called Rob to let him know what was going on. He managed to get a shot of Anna and Denado on the balcony together, so that's a plus."

"Was a bug placed in Anna's suite?" Holly asked.

"That was our intention, but Rob hasn't gotten the chance. Nick has a security officer watching the floor, and although Denado has been going in and out, Anna hasn't left the suite. I also called all the major operatives to tell them we have the painting. I don't think I have to tell you they are overjoyed. They've agreed to keep the good news away from the media until we have Denado and Anna in custody. I called Max, too, and Canna Makowa. She should be here anytime."

Holly frowned. "Canna Makowa, the artist?"

142 *Georgette Livingston*

"Uh-huh. An artist with a unique, little-known sideline. She can paint a copy of a painting that would make even the most astute art critic scratch his head and wonder which was the original. She's going to spend the night copying the painting, using a special quick-dry medium. She has until morning to finish the job, because a courier will be arriving first thing to take the original to Oahu. From there, it will be sent to Paris."

"Is Mario in any kind of trouble for keeping the painting all this time?"

"No, because of the special circumstances. They were talking like he might even get a reward."

"Well, he could certainly use the money. Okay, so what are we going to do with the copy?"

Logan grinned, exposing one elongated dimple. "As soon as it's finished and dry enough to handle, it will be mounted and framed, with the lithograph on top. Ty will take it to the house in Hanapepe, along with some of Mario's things. And then you're going to call Anna and tell her that although you haven't found Mario, you've found the house where he was staying. You can tell her all of his things are there, including a wonderful lithograph. That ought to get her attention. You can also tell her

Elima 143

that Mario owes back rent, and the landlord has locked up the house until he gets his money. My guess is, getting their hands on the painting will take priority over Mario, and they'll devise some creative plan to get it out of the house.''

"And you'll be waiting.''

"That's right, but there is one problem. There is always an outside chance they won't attempt the heist together. Denado could go alone, and we want Anna, too. Or vice versa. If that happens, we'll keep whoever it is under surveillance. We don't think they'll waste any time getting off the island, and we should be able to catch them together at the airport, with the painting.''

"What if they charter a boat, or a private plane?'' Holly asked.

"We have that covered. All the charter companies have been alerted, along with the airport. There won't be a boat or a plane available.''

"They could change their names.''

"We've handed out the photos.''

"They could swipe a boat.''

"Yes, they could, but remember, we'll be right behind them. Max has a few men he can spare, and we can use all the help we can get.''

Holly fluttered her eyelashes at him. "Does that include me?''

144 *Georgette Livingston*

"As a matter of fact, it does. I want you and Buzzy to cover the hotel, in case one of them stays behind. Anna doesn't know Buzzy, so he can keep an eye on the lobby. You can take Rob's place in the suite."

"And Rob?"

"He'll cover the airport until we get there."

"So that leaves you, Ty, and Coop to cover the house."

"That's right, and we'll have Max and his men for backup. Actually, I wish we had an army of agents, but nobody else is free. So it's up to us."

"The whole thing actually sounds easy," Buzzy muttered, "but I wonder if it is."

Ty spoke up. "None of it is ever easy, Buzzy, so the best thing to do is concentrate on the job, and see that it gets done."

Coop nodded. "And we usually get the job done."

"We'll all be carrying radios, and Max will clear a channel so we can keep in contact without interference, and without having to go through dispatch. By the way, did you call Cindy?"

Holly nodded. "I called her from the cellular on our way home. I didn't go into details. Just said Mario was here, and we had everything under control."

Elima 145

"And Jack?"

"I got the answering machine when I called the office, so I called him at home. Kim said he got a lead on the insurance scam, and went to Oahu for the day. You haven't said, Logan, but where is Mario going to be while all this is going down?"

"Right here, keeping Tutu company. I'll show him how to use the radio in the wine cellar so he can keep informed, but under no circumstances is he to leave the house."

Holly tittered. "Not much chance of that with Tutu in charge. Right now, he's in the kitchen helping her with dinner."

Logan grinned. "Speaking of dinner, I think we should put this on hold for an hour or so, and enjoy Tutu's offerings. Tomorrow night might be a whole different story."

"We're eating on the terrace," Holly said, leading the way.

Dinner was over, but they were still on the terrace, drinking cups of Kona coffee, when Canna Makowa arrived. She was a pretty island woman with a wide smile, and after introductions, Logan took her downstairs.

"Think she can really make a copy that'll pass inspection?" Buzzy asked after they'd gone.

146   *Georgette Livingston*

"Doesn't have to be perfect," Ty said. "More than likely, they'll wait until dark to make their move, and they won't take the time for a detailed inspection. Might remove the frame and lift up a corner of the lithograph, but that's about all."

"You keep saying 'they,'" Holly said. "Like you expect them to be together when they take the painting."

"Have to be ready if that happens," Coop said. "If that's the way they work it, we'll get them at the house. We've got it covered, Holly, so relax."

Holly exchanged glances with Buzzy, and she knew what he was thinking. There was no way anybody could relax. Not until Analisa Newfall and Frank Denado were behind bars.

While the men played cards in the garden room to help pass the time, Holly helped Tutu with the dishes, ignoring her protests. Finally, wearily, Holly went downstairs to see how the painting was going.

Canna Makowa looked up from the easel and smiled. "Three more hours at the most, Mrs. West, and I will be finished. This is an easy painting to copy, and fortunately, it is small. Maybe eight inches by eleven, and the style is very clean."

Elima 147

It was the first time Holly had seen the painting, and it was breathtakingly beautiful. Painted in shades of blue with touches of yellow and green, it was a summer scene set in dense woods, and it looked so real, she could actually see herself walking through the dappled sunlight as it shone through the trees.

"It's a lovely painting, Miss Makowa, and you do lovely work. I don't think I could tell it from the original."

"Trained eyes would know the difference," Canna said.

"Do you do your own paintings?" Holly asked.

"Yes, but my style is my own. Nothing like this."

"Did my husband tell you why we are doing this?"

Canna shook her head. "No, and I didn't ask. I've learned to do the work without asking questions. I'm not asked to do this sort of thing very often, but it's always a pleasure. It gives me the opportunity to wonder what it would be like to be a great master, and dream."

"Do you sell your paintings?"

"Occasionally I will have a show on Oahu. Most of the time, I do it for fun and relaxation."

148 *Georgette Livingston*

"One of the men upstairs is an artist," Holly said.

Canna's dark eyes twinkled. "The man with the beard. He came down earlier to take a peek, and was very interested in my work."

Holly noted the water pitcher on the table, and said, "Do you need anything before I turn in for the night?"

"No, I'm fine."

The door opened, and Holly looked up as Logan descended the stairs. "Is the card game over?" she asked, going into his arms.

He gave her a hug. "No, but I was losing my shirt. Are you going to bed soon? You look tired."

"I'm on my way. You?"

"Just as soon as Canna is finished with the painting." He smiled at the artist. "You're doing a great job, Canna."

Canna flushed and nodded. "Three more hours at the most, and it has been my pleasure."

Upstairs, Holly and Logan parted with a kiss, because Logan didn't expect her to be awake when he came to bed. But Holly doubted that she would be able to sleep. It was all coming down tomorrow. Just a few short hours away.

* * *

Elima 149

Sunlight streamed through the window when Holly awoke the next morning, and one look at the clock sent her into a frenzy. It was almost eleven! What on earth had Logan been thinking of to let her sleep so long? She didn't remember Logan coming to bed, and now, looking at the smooth sheets and pillow on his side of the bed, she wondered if he had.

Holly slipped into a muumuu and hurried down the hall. Not a sound, except for Tutu singing in the kitchen.

"Where is everybody?" Holly asked, rubbing her eyes. "And why didn't somebody wake me up!"

Tutu poured a cup of coffee, handed it to Holly, and clucked her tongue. "That bad man is dead, *nani* Holly. Word came early this morning. Found him in an elevator at the hotel. Two bullets, maybe three."

Holly's jaw dropped. "Frank Denado?"

"Denado, yeah. *Kāne* Logan wanted you to rest, and not be disturbed."

Holly ran a hand through her tangled hair. "Darn it! I'm not sorry the man is dead, but this messes everything up! All our plans . . ."

Tutu shook her head. "*Kāne* Logan said the plan is the same, only now they will be dealing with only one bad guy."

150   *Georgette Livingston*

"Anna. Wow, do you suppose she killed him?"

Tutu shrugged. "*Kāne* Logan also said for you to wait until he gets home before you make the call to Anna."

"And when might that be? If he's in the middle of a murder investigation . . . Where is Mario?"

"Downstairs, waiting to hear some news on the cop radio."

Holly gritted her teeth as anger mounted. There was no justifiable reason why Logan couldn't have taken the time to wake her up. There was no reason why she couldn't have been a part of this. She had been in on it from the beginning, after all, and was going to be a part of the finale. Or was she? Did Logan have some scheme up his sleeve to keep her at home until this was over? She loved him, she adored him, but sometimes he could be impossible! And what about Anna? If she killed Frank Denado, would she panic and run? Had they thought about that? Where would their plan be then? They couldn't simply walk into her suite and arrest her. Nor could they even approach her, if they were still going to go through with their original sting. Anna had no idea they knew about Denado, or that she was under sur-

Elima 151

veillance. Or that they had Mario and the painting.

Holly went to the phone and called Rob at the hotel. When it rang twenty times and he didn't answer, she hung up and fumed. "That's it! Everybody is out tending to Frank Denado's murder, while Anna could be on her way to the mainland!" She closed her eyes and tried to think. Nick. She had to call Nick!

Nick answered on the third ring, and sounded out of breath.

"Well, at least *you're* where you're supposed to be," she snapped. "Could you please tell me what's going on?"

"Utter madness," Nick said. "The hotel is crawling with cops, the guests are as mad as hornets, and nobody can get in or out of the hotel. I knew there would be days like this when I went into the business, but heck, I don't have to like it."

Holly sighed. "Have you seen my husband?"

"He left about an hour ago."

"Alone?"

"No, he was with Lt. Kentaro and a bunch of guys. Agents, I think, and one big dude with wild blond hair and freckles. They were on their way to the morgue. Said they wanted a

152   *Georgette Livingston*

fast autopsy, and an even faster ballistics report."

"What about Rob Miller? I just called the suite, but he didn't answer."

"He went with Logan."

"Wonderful. So who is watching Anna Rocettie's suite?"

"A cop and a hotel security officer. Like I said, the hotel is crawling with cops."

"Uh-huh, well, if Anna Rocettie is as smart as I think she is, she can get by an army of cops, and hotel security, without batting an eye."

"Want me to call Logan at the morgue?"

"No, if I wanted to talk to Logan, I'd make the call myself. Right about now, he doesn't want to hear what I have to say. I'll call you in a few minutes, Nick. Stay by the phone."

Holly walked to the window and looked out over the parking area. All the vehicles were there except Ty's silver Blazer. One vehicle, four conniving men, who were more concerned with Frank Denado's murder than catching Analisa Newfall. If she got away without the painting, Mario's life would forever be in danger.

Holly turned to Tutu, and managed a smile. "I take it the courier picked up the painting this morning?"

Elima 153

"He did, and everybody breathed a sigh of relief to have it out of the house, yeah."

"Is the copy still in the wine cellar?"

"*Kāne* Logan put it in his office. It is dry, but still has to be mounted."

"Okay. Well, I'm going to the police station, Tutu. Logan is there with his friends, and I have to ask them some questions."

Tutu frowned. "You just told that man on the phone you didn't want to talk to *kāne* Logan."

"I don't want to *talk* to him, I want to ask questions."

Before Tutu could blink, or protest, Holly hurried down the hall.

Chapter Nine

Holly waited until she was on the highway, and made sure that nobody was following her—it would be just like Logan to leave a stray behind to keep an eye on *her*—before she placed the call to Nick on the cellular phone.

"It's been longer than a few minutes," he said when he heard her voice.

"Sorry, but I wanted to wait until I was in my car. I'm approaching Kealia, doing seventy. Traffic is light. What's going on at the hotel?"

"Same old same. Cops everywhere. Everybody wants to check out. Gotta say, they aren't happy they can't. We're giving out free dinners and bottles of champagne, trying to keep the

Elima

155

guests happy. Got plainclothes detectives from Oahu, too. Big, tough-looking dudes. So you're in your car. Headed where?''

"I'm on my way to the hotel. Is there a way I can get in without anybody knowing?''

"Come on, Holly, I told you the hotel is swarming with cops, and nobody is getting in or out.''

"I know, but you own the hotel, Nick. You know every nook and cranny.''

"Well, I guess you could try the underground tunnel.''

"The tunnel that leads from the Orchid Lounge to the terrace pool?''

"Yeah. They've only got one cop out by the pool, but I don't know . . .''

"I'm creative, Nick, and it sounds perfect.''

"Should I ask what you're planning to do?''

"No, you shouldn't. Does the cop or the security officer watching Anna have a key card to her suite?''

"No.''

"Well, forget the cop. He'd ask too many questions. But make sure the security officer has a key, and tell him to listen for trouble.''

"Oh come on, Holly . . .''

"Tell him if he hears screams, or shouts, to use the key, and come in with his gun drawn.''

Nick groaned. "This is crazy.''

156 *Georgette Livingston*

"Maybe, but a man's life is at stake."

"Sounds like yours might be, too."

"I'd like to think I'm smarter than Anna Rocettie, and I'm going to prove it. I'm passing Wailua. You've got just enough time to talk to the security officer and give him a key. And tell him to zip his mouth."

Ten minutes later, Holly pulled into a secluded area at the northeast corner of the hotel and parked where the Blazer couldn't be seen from the road. With adrenaline pumping through her, and nearly breathless at the thought of what she was about to do, she shed her clothing, down to the bathing suit, and donned a beach jacket. She was wearing zories, and clopped along, keeping one eye on the road. The only stop she made was at the small fountain near the rear parking area, and that was only long enough to get herself wet, including her hair. After wrapping her head in a small towel she carried in her tote, she continued on. It wasn't a brilliant plan, but it was the only one she could come up with, and it had to work! The whole idea was to tell Anna about the house in Hanapepe, show her the painting, convince her Mario was really dead, and then see what happened. Holly couldn't think beyond that, and didn't want to. "Wing-

Elima 157

ing it'' had never been her mode of operation, and she didn't like the feeling of uncertainty.

The Kauai Terrace was a very large, opulent hotel, with several swimming pools. And although the pool on the terrace was the one she wanted, Holly had to think of something to explain her presence to the cop, because he would surely want to know why she wasn't sequestered away in the hotel like the rest of the guests.

She was nearing the terrace pool now, and could see the cop pacing back and forth. But instead of continuing on, she turned to the left and followed the dense tree line east for quite a distance, and then cut over to the beach. She looked back, could barely see the cop, and gave a satisfied sigh. Though the beach was deserted, colorful umbrellas had been left everywhere, dotting the sand like sugar candy on a cake. She picked one up, closed it, and dragged it along behind her.

Holly had reached the terrace and climbed the steps before the cop noticed her, and his reaction was just what she expected. And she was prepared.

''Miss, you can't go in the hotel.'' He was tall, dark, and young, and gave her a helpless shrug. ''Sorry.''

Holly pulled herself up to her full height of

158 *Georgette Livingston*

five feet, ten inches and demanded, "What do you mean, I can't go in the hotel? And where is everybody? I was *way* down the beach. Must have fallen asleep. I woke up, realized I was alone, and for a minute there, I thought I was having a bad dream. It looked like something right out of a science fiction movie. Did the Martians come down and zap everybody up in a flying saucer, or what?"

"I'm surprised you didn't hear the announcement over the loudspeaker," he said. "Everybody was told to go inside the hotel."

"Why?"

"I'm not at liberty to go into details, but there has been some trouble."

"Trouble?" Holly wailed. "Oh, no, it's a hurricane, isn't it! I saw all those clouds this morning, and—Oh, no! My husband is in the hotel, and I'm out here! He must be worried sick!"

"It's not a hurricane," the cop said, adjusting the collar on his shirt, like it was suddenly too tight around his neck.

Holly sat down on a bench and held her head in her hands. Her shoulders shook as deep cries ripped from her throat.

"Miss . . . Uh, well, you say your husband is in the hotel?"

Holly kept her head down. "We've only

Elima 159

been married a week. What am I going to do? He's probably with the hotel manager right now, trying to get some answers. Nobody loses a new wife. *He* wanted to go to Maui, but oh, no, I insisted we come here. Oh, dear, what am I going to do?''

"Ahem, well, I guess it wouldn't hurt to let you in. I guess you know how to get through the tunnel."

Holly stood up, rubbed her eyes, and gave him a brilliant smile. "Thank you, Officer . . ." She looked at his name tag. ". . . Officer Downs. I'm so grateful. You don't mind if I leave the umbrella here, do you?"

Before he could reply, or change his mind, Holly swept by him and hurried toward the entrance to the tunnel.

It wasn't a long tunnel, but it was dank and creepy. Holly listened to her echoing footsteps, and breathed a sigh of relief when she reached the steps that led to the Orchid Lounge, and heard all the jabbering voices. Most of the patrons sounded upset, and that would work to her advantage.

Holly peeked around the corner, then plunged into the sea of glumness. Most of the patrons were too busy drinking and lamenting their woes to give her a second glance, and she quickly made her way to the lobby. She'd

160   *Georgette Livingston*

planned to keep close to the potted palm trees until she reached the bank of elevators, but that wasn't necessary either. The lobby was full of angry, protesting guests, and a good many of them looked as bedraggled as she did. She fit right in.

Keeping an eye open for anybody she might know, or who might know her, Holly worked her way through the crowd, thankful she still had the towel on her head. Bright-red hair like a beacon, but not today.

At the end of the bank of elevators, one elevator had been sealed off with yellow Mylar tape, and cops were milling around. Suits, too, who Holly assumed were police detectives from Oahu.

Wondering who found the body, and feeling sorry for whoever had, Holly punched in Nick's access code to his private elevator. She was thankful he'd given it to her months before, and was waiting for the door to open, when one of the detectives approached her.

"What do you think you're doing?" he snapped.

Once again, Holly pulled herself up to her full height, met his dark, angry scowl, and snapped back, "I'm the hotel owner's girlfriend, if it's any of your business."

"Yeah, right. Well, for your information,

Elima 161

that's an express elevator to the penthouse, and can only be accessed by code.''

At that moment, the elevator door opened, and Holly gave the detective a fetching smile. ''I know,'' she purred, ''and I've got the code.''

The man's mouth was still hanging open as the elevator door closed behind her. Within seconds, it opened again, and Holly walked into Nick's plush, sterilely modern penthouse. It looked exactly as she remembered it. White furniture, silk flowers and plants, lots of glass and mirrors. There was no sign of Nick, of course, but then she wasn't expecting to see him. Poor Nick. He was probably down in his office, pulling his hair out, and wishing he'd never gotten into the hotel business.

Holly used the phone in the living room, and called Nick's office. He answered on the first ring. ''Yeah, now what!''

Holly grinned. ''It's me, Nick. I'm in your penthouse, but I'll be darned if I know where to go from here.''

''Holly? For Pete's sake, how did you manage that?''

''With your access code and some fancy talking. Any idea how I can get to Anna's suite from here?''

''For Pete's sake. Well, there is a door off

162 *Georgette Livingston*

the kitchen that leads to a stairwell, but I don't see how you're gonna get by the cop and security.''

''Can't you handle that? I mean, can't you call them down to your office?''

''And what am I going to tell 'em when they get here?''

''Hmm. How about if you tell 'em to be on the watch for a tall gal in a wet bathing suit with her head wrapped in a towel?''

''For Pete's sake!''

''Come on, Nick. Be an angel. You don't have to detain them long. They can be back at their posts in five minutes.''

''Don't you suppose they might ask me why I couldn't give them that information over the walkie-talkie?''

''Tell them the gal in the wet bathing suit with her head wrapped in a towel might have a walkie-talkie, too, and might be listening in.''

''For Pete's sake!''

''When this is over, I owe you a dinner, Nick. *Aloha*.''

''Holly ... Are you really wearing a wet bathing suit, and is your head really wrapped in a towel?''

''You betcha. Talk to you soon.'' She hung up before he could say ''For Pete's sake'' again, and headed for the kitchen.

Elima 163

By the time Holly reached Anna's floor, her heart was beating so hard, it sounded like a kettledrum pounding in her ears. *Still time to back out,* she kept telling herself as she opened the door to the hallway. But she also kept telling herself she had come too far, and too much was at stake.

There was no sign of the cop or the security officer in the hallway, and she took a deep breath. She had five minutes, maybe less.

When she reached Anna's suite, she knocked, and prayed. If the woman had already skipped out . . .

Anna opened the door. Her heart-shaped mouth opened, and a little gasp escaped from her throat. "I-I thought it was somebody from the hotel. Things have been in a terrible mess . . ."

"Tell me about it," Holly said, breezing into the room. "I was visiting some friends who are saying at the hotel, and we went out for a swim. And wouldn't you know? We'd barely gotten in the water, when we were told to get out and go inside. And then, well, can you just believe it? Somebody was murdered, and now nobody can get in or out of the hotel. Oh, I know, you're probably wondering why I was visiting friends and loafing around instead

164 *Georgette Livingston*

of looking for your husband, but . . . Well . . . Oh, dear, this is so difficult.''

''What's difficult?'' Anna managed to get out.

''*Everything!*'' Holly said, waving an arm. ''Anyway, my friends were in such a snit over the turn of events, I just couldn't take it. So I decided to come up here and see how you're doing. I was going to stop by anyway, because I have something to tell you . . .'' Holly took a deep breath. ''Well, getting up here wasn't easy. Cops are swarming all over the hotel. You take one step, and they want to know where you're going, and why. And if you can believe this, I even saw some detectives from Oahu. But boy, I can't figure that one out. A murder is a murder is a murder. Unless, of course, the victim was some VIP.''

While she rattled on, Holly took inventory. Anna was wearing an off-white knit dress and pumps, and her bags were sitting near the door. There were also damp spots on the sky-blue carpeting. Blood spots? Had she removed them with water, or club soda? Had she actually killed Frank Denado? If so, had she killed him in the suite, and then stuffed him into the elevator? Not likely. Anna was a small woman, and Denado was a large man. She probably shot him in the suite, and then he staggered

Elima 165

out. Maybe she opened the elevator door and gave him a little shove, knowing he would be dead before the elevator reached the next floor. Did she use her gun, or his? Probably his. Had to have used a silencer, or Rob would have heard the shots. Two shots, maybe three. That's what Tutu said. No signs of the gun now, but Anna's handbag was on the table next to the couch.

"I see you're packed and dressed for travel," Holly went on. "Can't blame you. Half the guests in the hotel want to leave. Unfortunately, everybody is stuck, including me."

Anna sat down in a chair and ran a hand through her dark hair. "It-it's really terrible."

"Yes, it certainly is. Have you decided what hotel you're going to stay in after you can get out of here? Better let me know, so I can keep in touch."

"I don't know. I haven't thought about it . . ."

Anna's eyes were darting around, and she was beginning to look like a caged animal. Holly sat down on the couch, within arm's length of Anna's handbag and the phone. Her own tote was by her side.

"Well, I guess now isn't the time to tell you this, what with the hotel in such a turmoil, and no way to leave, and it's the real reason I went

166 *Georgette Livingston*

to see my friends first. I was trying to get up the courage to talk to you . . . Oh, dear, this is so difficult.''

Anna gave Holly an impatient scowl. "Please, Miss St. James.''

''I found out where your husband is staying . . . Maybe I should change that to *was* staying. The landlord hasn't seen him in days, and the police have a body at the morgue . . . Well, I know they have the body of the murder victim, but I mean *another* body, who fits your husband's description. Of course, it was in the water for a long time, and . . . Oh, dear. I'm so very, very sorry, Anna. I know this must be a terrible, terrible shock. The police will eventually get a positive I.D., so we'll know, one way or the other. Meanwhile, I have all Mario's stuff. I know that might sound a little unorthodox, but the property room at the police station was filled to capacity, and they know they can trust me.''

Color drained from Anna's face, and her body grew rigid. "You . . . you found his house?''

''Well, it isn't exactly a house. It's just a little cottage out in the middle of nowhere.''

''Then how did you find it?''

''He left a trail of bread crumbs. In other words, once I picked up his trail, it was easy

Elima 167

to follow. You want a glass of water? Maybe a drink?''

Anna shook her head. "And . . . and you have his things?''

"Yes, I do. He didn't have much. Some clothing, some art supplies, a few books. I have everything in one box in a closet at home. Oh, and this! I brought it along because I thought it looked expensive, and I wanted your opinion. If it is expensive, I have to find a safe place to keep it, because I certainly don't want to toss it in the closet.''

Holly reached into her tote, bypassed the .38, and pulled out the folder that contained the painting. She pulled it out, moved closer to Anna so she could see it, but didn't hand it to her.

Anna's hands were shaking, and she clasped them in her lap. "It-it's lovely,'' she finally managed to say.

"Yes, it is. I'm not familiar with the artist, but perhaps you are?''

"Yes, I am, and it's *very* expensive.''

Holly returned to her seat, put the painting in her tote, and sighed. "Well, it's settled then. I'll take it to my bank, and they can put it in the safe.''

"I can take it,'' Anna said quickly. "I can put it in the hotel safe.''

168   *Georgette Livingston*

"I'm afraid that's impossible, Anna. Until the police identify the body, and have proof it was an accidental death—"

"I'm his wife!" Anna exclaimed.

"Yes, of course you are. But I don't make the rules. I simply follow them. I think you should try to relax, Anna. Maybe we should both have a glass of wine. Unless, of course, you're out. I know under normal circumstances, the hotel keeps the Robo bar well stocked, but with everything in such a mess . . ."

"I have wine," Anna said woodenly. "Why don't you pour it? I have to go to the bathroom."

The minute Anna went into the bedroom and closed the double doors behind her, Holly opened Anna's handbag. No gun. Was she in the bedroom, getting it? Was she going to come out firing a barrage of bullets?

Holly kept her tote over her shoulder, her .38 within easy reach, and walked to the bar. Her legs felt weak, and her heart pounded. Telling herself Anna wouldn't be that stupid, because there was no way she could get rid of another body with cops lurking around every corner, she tried to take some of her own advice. She had to relax with this, and try to outsmart Anna. *Analisa,* she reminded herself.

Elima 169

Girlfriend and accomplice of the notorious Frank Denado. And now Denado was dead. That definitely put Anna in a different light.

Holly was sitting on the couch when Anna walked in, wearing a nubby brown thigh-length jacket with big slash pockets and a tulip-shaped hem. It was very pretty, and stylish, but totally out of place. You didn't wear jackets in the islands. You wore them in San Francisco, where even the summers were cool. Nor did you try to hide a gun in a pocket when you were in the same room with a P.I. For someone so cunning, Anna could also be stupid sometimes.

Anna sat down in the chair and picked up the glass of wine Holly had placed on the nearby table. She took a sip, and shrugged. ''I know it probably sounds silly, but I'm freezing to death.''

''Probably the shock of it all,'' Holly said, noting the way the jacket shifted to one side from the weight of the gun.

''Probably.''

Anna's face resembled a piece of granite, but Holly could see the expression in her eyes. The woman wanted the painting, and was plotting her next move. And so was Holly. She wondered what would happen if she simply got

170 *Georgette Livingston*

up and walked out. Would that force Anna's hand? If so, what then?

Reminding herself Anna wouldn't chance killing her here, and that she wouldn't accomplish anything by pulling the gun and demanding the painting, because there was no place to go, Holly said, "I suppose I should call my husband and tell him I'm here."

Anna's eyes glittered. "Your husband doesn't know you're here?"

"No. Uh-oh, I forgot. He's over on Maui on business today. Well, maybe I should call the police station, and find out how the investigation is going. Better yet, I think I'll call the owner of the hotel, and put on some pressure. He's supposed to be a good friend, and I think it's time I put friendship to the test. Surely, there is *something* he can do to get us out of here. I've certainly helped him out of some tough spots."

"If we do get out, where will we go?" Anna asked casually.

Just as casually, Holly replied, "Well, first of all, I'll take the painting to the bank, and then we can hang out at the police station. Or we can go to my house. Or I can show you some sights to kill some time. I don't think it really matters where we go, just as long as we get out of here!"

Elima 171

Holly had no intentions of going anywhere with Anna. She was aware that once they were in the car, Anna would make her move, putting Holly at a disadvantage because she would be driving. But she needed the ruse to check in with Nick. And Anna fell for it.

"So call the hotel owner," Anna said impatiently.

Holly picked up the phone and punched in Nick's private number. He answered on the first ring, and sounded nearly frantic. "Hi, Nick," Holly said. "It's Holly—"

"Thank goodness! This has been one crazy half hour."

"I know how you feel. Just getting around the hotel is a nightmare."

"You know darn well that's not what I mean."

"I know, and I understand, but you *are* the owner, after all."

"Uh-huh, so you can't talk. I take it you made it to Anna's suite?"

"That's right. I'm visiting a client, Nick, and we're both going a little crazy. Isn't there *something* you can do to get us out of the hotel?"

"Okay, I'll talk, and you listen. You're gonna kill me, but after you called me the sec-

172   *Georgette Livingston*

ond time—when you were on the highway—I called Logan.''

Holly grimaced, but managed to keep her wits about her. ''And?''

''Logan and his group of merrymakers arrived at the hotel before you did. Here, somebody wants to talk to you.''

Holly looked at Anna, sighed, and shrugged.

''Holly, this is Coop. No time for details. Logan, Rob, Ty, and Buzzy are in the suite next to Anna's. Cops by the zillions out in the hall.''

''Well, I still think there must be a way,'' Holly said. ''Come on, Nick. Think about all the things I've done for you.''

''I'm on the radio right now with Logan,'' Coop said. ''They are on Anna's balcony, near the bedroom. Drapes are closed. Are you in the bedroom?''

''No.''

''Does Anna have a gun?''

''Yes, I know, but you're supposed to be the boss. You know, it's too bad I don't have rapelling gear in my pocket. Then we could go over the balcony and escape from this crazy place.'' She looked at Anna and rolled her eyes.

''Okay, the gun is in Anna's pocket. Is she aware you know she has it?''

Elima 173

"Not on your life! I refuse to spend one night here!"

"Where are you, exactly?"

"Look, Nick, I'm sitting on the couch, twiddling my thumbs. We have things to do and places to go."

"And Anna?"

"No, I wouldn't be more comfortable in a chair, and you're changing the subject."

"She's sitting in a chair. Facing the balcony?"

"Yes. I know. This is making you an old man."

"It sure as heck is. The balcony doors are open. You've got to get her turned around, so her back is to the balcony."

"Okay, I can wait."

"You're going to put the phone down, but you don't want me to hang up."

"I said I can wait, Nick, just don't take all day."

Holly held the receiver in her hand, and shook her head. "He said he has to check on something before he can give me a yes or a no. If he says no, I'm going to strangle him!"

"Where is your car?" Anna asked, watching Holly intently.

"Parked near the rear lot, under a stand of

174 *Georgette Livingston*

trees. I hate to get into a hot car, so I always try to find the shadiest spot.''

Holly's heart was pounding so hard, she was sure Anna could hear it. Worse, she had no idea how she was going to get the woman's back to the balcony.

She put the phone to her ear, waited a few minutes, and said, ''Then the answer is no?''

Coop said, ''She doesn't have her back to the balcony. Okay, let's try this. I'll contact one of the cops in the hall, and have him knock on the door. While Anna is talking to him, Logan and the others can gain entry. Stay out of the way, Holly, in case there is an exchange of gunfire.''

''Well, thanks for nothing,'' Holly snapped, and slammed down the phone. She shook her head. ''I guess you could tell he isn't going to cooperate. Darn!'' And then she smiled slyly. ''Guess we could always try the rapelling bit with sheets tied together.''

Anna wasn't smiling.

Seconds later, a knock sounded at the door. When Anna looked hesitant, Holly said, ''Probably the maid. You don't have the DO NOT DISTURB sign out, so if you don't open the door, she will.''

Reluctantly, Anna trudged to the door. Holly remained on the couch, out the line of fire, and

Elima 175

what happened next was like a scene in an action movie. Swift, professional, and effective.

The cop at the door smiled at Anna, and said, "Sorry to bother you, miss, but we're talking to all the guests. Just have a few questions to ask you . . ."

Anna cursed. "Haven't we been put through enough?"

"Yes, ma'am, but . . ."

Holly didn't hear the rest of it. She saw shadows on the balcony first, and then there they were, four of the most beautiful men she had ever seen. Before Anna realized what was happening, Logan was behind her with his .45 in her back. The cop drew his weapon, and almost on cue, the hallway was filled with uniformed cops and detectives.

"Nice and easy, Analisa Newfall," Logan said as he brought her hands behind her back and cuffed her. The pat-down came next, and the gun. The biggest "Dirty Harry" gun Holly had ever seen.

"Uh-huh, and the gun cuts it," Logan said. "I think we have a match. You're under arrest for the murder of one Frank Denado. You have the right to remain silent . . ."

While Logan read Anna her Miranda rights, she whirled around, spewing out obscenities

176   *Georgette Livingston*

while she glared at Holly. "You witch! You set me up!"

Holly got up on shaky legs, and although she tried to match Anna's rancor, her voice sounded shaky, too. She leaned against Buzzy for support. "Just like you set Mario up in San Francisco." She reached into her tote and pulled out the painting. "I know it looks like the original, but it isn't. The original is on its way to Paris as we speak. Oh, and about Mario. He isn't dead. Right now, he's waiting for news. The wonderful news that it's over, and he can get on with his life."

High color had replaced the pallor in Anna's face, but she didn't comment, except to say, "I want a lawyer."

Logan chuckled. "Oh, you'll get a lawyer, lady, and the best cell on Oahu. Nice and roomy, with lots of ventilation through the bars." He nodded at the army of cops. "Get her out of here."

Max poked his head in the door. "We gotta go through the room, Logan."

Logan nodded. "Give us a minute."

When the door closed, and they were alone, Holly flew into Logan's arms and wept tears of relief while he kissed her and scolded her, and shed a few tears, too.

Elima 177

"It was a crazy stunt, Holly," he said finally, "but . . ."

She looked up at him through her tears, and said, "Nick said he called you after I called him. Said you got to the hotel before I did. So why didn't you try to stop me? I'm sure he told you about the tunnel. It was the only logical way to get in, only one cop to deal with . . ."

Logan gave her an impish grin. "We knew about the tunnel, and Officer Downs had instructions to let you in. You were watched every minute, my love, and although we had no idea what you hoped to gain by this, we decided to let you play it out."

Holly shook her head. "You could have told me."

"No, we couldn't, because the less you knew the better. There was always the chance you'd let something slip out inadvertently, and put your life in real jeopardy."

"And my life wasn't in *real* jeopardy?"

"Of course it was. And it won't be the last time. We are who we are, sweetheart, and that isn't going to change."

Holly shook her head. "No, it isn't, but I swear, I'm never going to be able to think like a cop. Frank Denado was shot and stuffed in the elevator. If you suspected Anna, why didn't

178 *Georgette Livingston*

you pick her up right away? That's the reason I concocted this crazy scheme in the first place. When I woke up this morning and found out what had happened, and that you were at the morgue, more interested in a dead body than Anna getting away— Well, I just couldn't believe it, and I knew I had to do something! I called Nick from the house, and he said there was a cop and a security officer watching Anna's suite. One cop, and one security officer!''

Logan rained soft kisses over Holly's brow. ''She wasn't going anywhere without the painting, and that's the reason we didn't pick her up. Frank Denado was a mobster, with a lot of enemies. There was always the possibility somebody else killed him, and if we had picked up Anna before we knew for sure, and if she *wasn't* the killer, we would've had to let her go. At that point, she would've taken off for sure, and any chance we had for setting up the painting heist would've gone right along with her. So, my love, as it turned out, your way was best. Sure, there was always the chance she wasn't the killer, or if she was, she'd gotten rid of the gun, but you're a first-class detective, Holly, and that's what we were counting on.''

Holly pulled back, and glared up at him. ''So you just sat back while I had to jump

Elima 179

through fire, climb mountains, swim rivers, and machete my way through the jungle to get into the hotel and up here.''

''Ah, but it was worth it,'' Logan said, with his eyes flickering over her appreciatively. ''I haven't seen you in a bathing suit in a long time. You still have the sexiest legs on the island.''

''Compliments will get you everywhere,'' she said, resting her cheek against his chest. ''What now?''

''The cops will want your statement, but other than that, we can go home. We have a lot of celebrating to do.''

It was dark by the time Logan pulled Holly's Blazer into the parking area beside the house. Between the media blitz, giving Kauai P.D. a statement, and answering the detectives' one hundred and one questions, they'd gotten away from the hotel later than expected. Ty and Coop had gone home from the hotel, and Rob was on his way to Oahu, but Buzzy had accepted their dinner invitation. Holly had given him a big hug when he'd said, ''Might as well. I have to pick up my car anyway,'' and then she'd teased him about being addicted to Tutu's cooking. But getting his car and Tutu's cooking weren't the only reasons he wanted to

180 *Georgette Livingston*

be with them on this special night. He wanted to be a part of the friendship they shared, and join in the celebration, because another case was solved, and it was simply good to be alive.

Tutu met them at the door, and although Logan had called earlier to give her the good news, her eyes were still bright with unshed tears.

"*Aloha*," she whispered huskily.

"*Aloha*," Holly said, giving her a hug. "Where is Mario?"

"Out on the terrace, fighting with that thing *kane* Logan calls a barbecue, because he got tired of watching *me* fight with it. We are barbecuing ribs, but now, I think roasting a pig in an *imu* would be easier, yeah."

Logan chuckled. "Guess we'd better give him a hand, Buzzy."

When they walked out on the terrace, Mario looked up from the grill, and gave them a sheepish shrug. "I never could get the hang of this barbecuing stuff, but I felt so sorry for Tutu . . ." Another shrug. "I've spent the last couple of hours trying to come up with some way to tell you how much I appreciate what you've done for me, because a simple thanks just doesn't seem adequate."

"A simple thanks is more than adequate," Holly said softly. "Because it's all part of the

Elima   181

job.'' She winked at Logan. ''It's who we are, and what we do, and we wouldn't have it any other way.''

Logan spoke up. ''You can spend the night here, Mario, and then in the morning, I'll take you to the police station.

Lt. Kentaro wants to ask you a few questions so he can finalize his report, but don't worry. It's only a formality.''

Buzzy cleared his throat. ''So, what are you gonna do now, Mario?''

''I have to settle my affairs in San Francisco, and then I'd like to come back to Kauai. Maybe that way, I can at least realize half my dream.''

Holly smiled. ''Like spending lazy days painting under a tropical sun? You are a very good artist, Mario, and your work would always be in demand. And I know one person who will be thrilled if that's what you decide to do.''

''Your friend, Cindy? I know. She called earlier, and said she had some money for me. I wanted to tell her to keep it, but I'll need it to get back to the mainland.''

''What about your paintings?'' Logan asked.

''She can sell them, or keep them. I really don't care. I created those paintings while I

182   *Georgette Livingston*

was under a lot of stress, and I know I can do a lot better.''

''What about your art gallery in San Francisco?'' Holly asked.

''I'm going to sell it, because it holds nothing but bad memories. Along with hiding out, I've had a lot of time to think, and I've decided it's time to take charge of my life. Do the things I really want to do, and worry about tomorrow, tomorrow. If nothing else, this whole thing has taught me that life is too short to squander it away.''

Just then, Tutu padded out to the terrace, carrying a tray of *pupus*, and her smile was wide and glowing. ''Figured those ribs won't be ready to eat until midnight, so you'd better have something to eat *wikiwiki*.''

Her comment brought smiles around, and added to the special moment.

''We have a lot to celebrate,'' Logan said, putting his hand out to Holly. ''Shall we get the champagne and glasses?''

With love filling her heart, Holly nodded and took his hand. He was her *kāne*, and her strength. Her life.

''*Aloha au ia oe*,'' she whispered softly as they made their way into the house. ''Forever and ever, and even after that.''

NORWALK PUBLIC LIBRARY
NORWALK OHIO
WITHDRAWN